Bat Out of Hell

Also in the Crime Classics series:

MY FRIEND MR CAMPION AND OTHER MYSTERIES
Margery Allingham

BLUEPRINT FOR MURDER
Roger Bax

DEATH WALKS IN EASTREPPS
Francis Beeding

TRIAL AND ERROR
Anthony Berkeley

THE PYTHON PROJECT
THE WHIP HAND
Victor Canning

MY BROTHER'S KILLER
Dominic Devine

THE TYLER MYSTERY
THE WORLD OF TIM FRAZER
Francis Durbridge

ALL THE LONELY PEOPLE
Martin Edwards

THE CASE OF THE CROOKED CANDLE
Eric Stanley Gardner

NO TEARS FOR HILDA
Andrew Garve

BEFORE THE FACT
Francis Iles

THROUGH A GLASS, DARKLY
Helen McCloy

WHO SAW HER DIE?
Patricia Moyes

CLOSE UP ON DEATH
Maureen O'Brien

SOME MUST WATCH
Ethel Lina White

Bat Out of Hell

AN INSPECTOR CLAY MYSTERY

FRANCIS DURBRIDGE

ABOUT THE AUTHOR

Francis Durbridge (1912-1998), most famous as the creator of Paul Temple, also wrote several non-series thrillers, of which this title is one of the best examples. The story was used as the basis of a successful 1966 BBC TV series of the same name, starring John Thaw and Sylvia Syms.

This edition published in the UK by Arcturus Publishing Limited
26/27 Bickels Yard, 151–153 Bermondsey Street, London SE1 3HA

Cover artwork by Steve Beaumont, coloured by Adam Beaumont
Typesetting by Couper Street Type Co.

AD002457EN

Printed in the UK

CHAPTER I

She could hear him in the room below, struggling with the locked suitcase and swearing loudly enough to be heard all over the house. It was hard to believe that only a few years ago the sound of that voice on the telephone had been enough to send delicious shivers down her spine. Geoffrey's voice, vibrant and caressing when it wanted to be, had been one of the things that had captivated her. Lately it had always seemed to harden when he spoke to her.

She moved to the bedroom window, unconsciously putting off the moment when she would have to go downstairs and say goodbye to him. It had started to rain again. A typical August morning in southern England. A few miles away across the fields the roofs of Alunbury glistened wetly in the grey light. She pulled the curtain clear of the window ledge and closed it.

The clothes she intended to pack for Cannes were laid out on the bed, their gay colours incongruous on this rainy day. She knew she would have to go ahead with her programme for the day, just as if she really believed that she and her husband would be taking off for their holiday in the south of France that evening. It was essential to appear calm and natural, though she knew that her mouth was unnaturally dry and her hands were trembling. She picked up the fur coat that had been thrown across the back of a chair, went out on to the landing and began to descend the staircase.

Even under stress, Diana Stewart moved with instinctive poise. Now in her early thirties, she had taken good care to preserve her looks. Her figure was, if anything, better than when she had been younger, for she had learned how to carry herself and how to stand and to sit so that her excellent shape showed to the best advantage. She wore clothes well and had an instinct for jewelry. The face which she presented to the world was one of carefree serenity, the devoted wife of a successful and prosperous husband. When she was alone or in an unguarded moment a certain tightening of the mouth and narrowing of the eyes betrayed the unfeminine streak in her nature, a ruthless determination to have things her own way.

Now, as she crossed the hall, she carefully composed her features, hiding her hands under the fur coat.

'Geoffrey,' she called. 'You're going to be late for the office. Do you want me to give you a hand with your packing?'

The answer was a grunt from the direction of the drawing room. She went to stand in the doorway.

He had an ancient leather suitcase balanced on the arm of a settee and was kneeling on the floor struggling unsuccessfully to unlock it. He glanced up and saw her watching him. Conscious perhaps of the ridiculousness of his posture he stood up. The suitcase slid off the arm on to the damask cushions of the settee.

Geoffrey Stewart was a tall, well-built man of about forty-seven. Prosperity had not improved his looks. Too much good living had thickened his waist-line and coarsened his features. But a head of unruly fair hair lent a certain youthfulness to his looks and the devil-may-care expression in his eyes still had the power to captivate women. And, of course, there was always that voice with which he could charm the birds off the trees. She often wondered how many other women he had used it on since they had been married and whether it was a sense of guilt that had made him so intolerant towards her.

Seeing him standing there in that slightly helpless and pitiful attitude reminded her of one of the first picnics when he had tried to light a fire in the woods and failed dismally. The memory made her heart turn over and tightened her throat. To cover her emotion she walked past him and put the fur coat down on an armchair. It was almost a relief when he addressed her in the bad-tempered voice to which she had grown accustomed.

'You're not proposing to take your mink coat with you.'

'Don't be ridiculous.' She spoke coldly over her shoulder. 'Thelma's picking it up. She's taking it to the furrier's for me. I'm having it altered while I'm away.'

She arranged the coat carefully on the chair, smoothing the glistening fur with her fingers before forcing herself to turn and look directly at him.

'That's right, Di,' he was saying. 'Spend every bob I've got. Never mind the cost.'

'I'm only having it altered.' She spoke the words with slow emphasis, as if explaining an evident truth to a child. 'And will you please stop calling me Di. You know I hate it.'

She nodded her blonde head at the suitcase. 'Well – have you found the key?'

'Yes. But it won't work. I think the lock's jammed.' He bent down and wrestled with the key again. 'Now I can't even get the bloody key out. Damned nuisance. We'll just have to make do with the two cases we've got upstairs. I expect there's room.'

She turned away and moved towards her writing desk which was in an alcove near the tall eighteenth-century windows. Their conversation was falling into the familiar pattern of thrust and counter-thrust.

'You could buy another suitcase.'

'Yes. I thought you'd say that. Buy – buy – buy. That's usually your solution, isn't it, Diana?'

'Oh, Geoffrey, for God's sake! You've had that case donkey's years. It looks like something out of the ark.'

'This case belonged to my father. It's solid leather. A damned sight better than the gimcrack stuff you can buy nowadays.'

'What good is it if you can't get it unlocked?' She had her back to him now and was opening the drawers of her desk one by one. They both heard the door-bell ring at the far end of the hall and the sound of four taps on the brass lion-head knocker of the front door.

'That's the front door. It's probably your friend Thelma.'

He had finally extracted the key from the suitcase and was standing there, the ring of keys dangling from his hand. He had managed to make even the remark about Thelma sound like an accusation.

'Well,' she retorted with annoyance, 'Mrs Houston can answer it.'

'Mrs Houston?' Puzzled, Geoffrey stared towards the hall, where prim feet were mincing towards the front door. 'But I thought she had already gone.'

'No,' Diana said casually. 'She changed her mind. She's catching the eleven o'clock. I said I'd run her to the station.'

She opened the last of the drawers and this time found what she was looking for, a pair of extra large Polaroid sunglasses with broad mock-tortoise-shell rims. She held them up against the light and noted with satisfaction that, thanks to the small tiff, her nerves had steadied down. Her hands had stopped trembling.

Behind her, at the doorway, she heard Mrs Houston's voice.

'Mr Paxton, sir.'

'Hello, Mark,' Geoffrey exclaimed. 'What do you want? It's nine o'clock. Why the devil aren't you at the office?'

She turned round with deliberate slowness, knowing that she must play this scene out with deadly control. Mrs Houston had withdrawn, closing the door behind the visitor. Mark Paxton was coming forward towards his employer, awkwardly holding a suitcase, made apparently of black leather. He was a young man in his late twenties, with dark good looks and wavy, black hair which was allowed to curl upward at the back of his head. He had allowed his sideboards to grow down level with the bottom of his ears. The grey suit he wore was dashingly cut and relieved by a bold pin-stripe. His waistcoat was a plushy maroon with mother-of-pearl buttons and his tie had come from the King's Road, Chelsea. Except in the presence of Geoffrey Stewart he was extremely self-possessed and confident.

'I thought perhaps you might like to borrow this, sir.'

He proffered the suitcase tentatively. His accent was very uppah-class, but somehow unconvincing, as if he had learnt it at a school of elocution. 'When we were talking about your holiday . . .'

He broke off and glanced towards Diana as if he had only just noticed that she was in the room. 'Oh, good morning, Mrs Stewart.'

'Good morning, Mark,' she said evenly. Their glances met briefly, then slid away again.

'Yes, yes, of course!' Geoffrey said. 'I remember now. But you shouldn't have taken me literally. I merely meant that . . .' He put out a hand and relieved the young man of the suitcase, shooting an embarrassed glance at his wife. 'I said we were a bit short on cases and Mark offered to help us out. Very kind of you, old chap, very kind.'

Geoffrey was examining the suitcase warily, as if he was about to buy it but hardly dared to ask the price. Inside, some small metallic object was rattling about.

'Looks just the job to me . . .'

'The keys are inside,' Mark explained.

'Yes, I can see that.'

There was an awkward pause. Diana tried her sunglasses on, adjusting them on the bridge of her nose as she looked out at the faintly lightening sky.

'Is there anything else I can do, sir? Perhaps I could run you and Mrs Stewart to the airport?'

'No, no. It's all laid on, thank you very much. Ned Tallboy's taking us.' Geoffrey laid Mark's suitcase down on the settee beside his own and patted the young man's arm encouragingly.

'I'll see you at the office, old chap. We're not leaving until this evening.'

Even when talking to another man, Diana thought, his voice was terribly attractive. It was odd that he could address one of his employees in a more civil tone than his own wife.

'I hope you have a pleasant journey, Mrs Stewart.'

Mark had turned towards her again. She took the sunglasses off and gave him a formal smile.

'Thank you.'

'And a lovely holiday. I'm sure you will. It was seventy-eight in Nice yesterday.'

He was holding the glance too long, yet she could not drag her own eyes away from Mark's. She wondered if he was trying to communicate some secret message to her.

'Seventy-eight!' Geoffrey exploded, breaking the momentary tension. 'Good grief, we'll fry!'

'Well, it's bound to be either too hot or not hot enough, isn't it, Geoffrey?' Diana went past Mark towards the settee, almost brushing against him in doing so. 'Thank you for the case, Mark – it's a very nice one. We'll take good care of it.'

'Yes, of course we will,' Geoffrey said briskly. 'He knows that. Come along, Mark.'

She heard the door open and knew that Geoffrey was shepherding Mark out into the hall, but she did not turn round until she was certain that he was out of view. Then she stood, staring at the empty space of the open door, her heart pounding in her breast.

She went to the coffee table in front of the marble fireplace and bent to take a cigarette from the box. The Wedgwood lighter was on the mantelpiece. She snapped it into flame and drew smoke deep into her lungs. Not much longer now. He'd soon be gone to the office and she would be on her own, relieved of the necessity to act out every remark and gesture of this unbearable pantomime.

From the hall came the sound of voices. Geoffrey had met someone at the front door and was bringing them in. She listened to their steps crossing the floor of the hall.

'She's in the drawing room,' Geoffrey's voice said. 'Go on in.'

Diana had herself under complete control as she faced the new visitor. Thelma Bowen looked exactly what she was, a successful business woman in her late thirties. Any man who had contemplated marrying her must have seen at a glance that it would be she who would wear the pants. She was heavily built, well padded with firm, rounded flesh. She was as vain as they come and spent money lavishly on her own person. The result was a little excessive for rural Alunbury. Thelma always looked as if she was about to set off for some risqué party in Mayfair.

'Geoffrey told me to come on in,' she said.

'Oh, hello, Thelma! How nice to see you!'

'Am I too early?'

'No, of course not.' Diana went to meet Thelma and kissed her on a fleshy, pink and faintly scented cheek. 'How are you? How's Walter?'

'Oh, Walter's all right. You know Walter. Lazy little devil.' Jingling bracelets, she plonked her massive handbag on the coffee table and moved towards the chair on which Diana had put her mink coat. 'Is that the coat, dear?'

'Yes, you know where to take it?'

'Bolton's in Cork Street.' Thelma had picked up the coat with loving reverence. She inclined her cheek and caressed it sensuously with the sleeve. 'I adore mink. Oh, some people don't know they're born. Why on earth didn't I marry a millionaire?'

'Geoffrey's not a millionaire,' Diana said with some asperity. She stubbed the half-smoked cigarette out in the ash-tray. 'And even if he was he'd still be mean as hell.'

'Oh, come off it. Mink coats, Aston Martins, four weeks in Cannes every year . . .'

'Yes, well – for your information I'm not allowed to drive the Aston, I saved up for the coat myself, and as for four weeks in Cannes!' Diana sank down into the armchair where lately her fur coat had lain. 'Do you know where we are staying?'

'The Carlton, I imagine.' Thelma had really taken possession of the mink coat now and was hugging it to her bosom and purring over it.

'The Carlton, my foot! We stay at the "Plage et Angleterre" and if you haven't heard of it I'm not surprised! Not that the hotel worries Geoffrey. He's usually on the golf course by ten o'clock.'

'Fancy going to Cannes to play golf,' Thelma said, her throaty chuckle bubbling up from her pneumatic chest. 'Does he wear a bikini?'

Diana's laughter echoed Thelma's but she realised with a shock that she had not got it under control, that she was very close to hysteria. Geoffrey's voice at the doorway sobered her.

'What's the joke?'

'You, darling. We're laughing at you.'

'Is that so?' Geoffrey's eyes switched from Diana to Thelma and back again. He looked far from amused. 'Well, I'm off to the office. I'll be back this afternoon about half past three. Ned's picking us up at five o'clock, so be ready.' He nodded to Thelma. 'Keep an eye on the place while we're away, Thelma.'

'Yes, all right, Geoff. Have a good time.'

He was gone. She heard his steps recede along the hall, then the sound of the Aston Martin starting up outside. By that time she had another cigarette in her mouth and was holding the flame to it. She realised that Thelma was staring at her.

'What's the matter, Diana? You just stubbed a cigarette out without finishing it and now you're lighting another. And your hand's trembling like a leaf.'

'It's nothing.' Diana shook her head. 'I'm always like this before a journey. Aeroplanes make me nervous. I'm scared stiff of them.'

There was nothing about Alunbury to suggest that it would make an ideal setting for murder. It seemed just a typical country town set in the English landscape some forty miles from London. The old and historic part of the township lay around the ancient Market Cross, once the meeting place of two Roman roads. But the building of a near-by motorway had brought Alunbury within easy commuting distance of

London. The value of property in the area was rising fast. Already a sprawl of new houses had spread over the hill to the north and the bulldozers were just moving on to what had once been parkland not a mile from the Market Cross. Despite a vigorous rearguard action by the Society for the Preservation of Rural Alunbury, a new multi-storey car park had thrust its concrete form into the skyline three hundred yards from the Cross, whilst the new police station, an ultra-modern purpose-built building, occupied the site of what had formerly been the cattle market.

Admittedly tempers ran high when the interest of those who wished to preserve the character of the town clashed with that of others who were determined to develop, rebuild and bring new industries to the area. But violence in Alunbury was a rarity. Its inhabitants clicked their tongues when they read about the vice and strife of the big cities, but in their hearts they knew that such things could never happen here. The only bodies which the local police had to pick up were the victims of accidents at one or other of the black spots in and around the town.

So, on this morning in August, Alunbury presented its usual placid appearance. A rain-cloud was moving across the county, dropping slightly angled shafts of grey on to the glistening green fields. The faint haze of smoke hung over the roof-tops, waiting for a mid-morning breeze to move it on. The confused hum of a small town going about its Monday business was broken by only one discordant note, that of the ambulance carving a way through the town centre towards the hospital on the outskirts. A private car had caught the tail-end of an articulated lorry turning into Carden's Automotive Components and the top of the coachwork had been sliced off. The driver of the car was killed instantly, but his passenger was, for the moment at any rate, alive. So the ambulance had all headlights on, its blue light flashing and its siren going full blast.

It was an occurrence dramatic enough to bring most activities in Alunbury to a halt. In her little sweet-shop in Station Road Miss Kitty Tracy stood on tip-toe behind her cabinet of gaily-wrapped sweets and chocolates to watch the white vehicle race past. It would not be long before she found out who was inside it. Not much happened in Alunbury without Miss Tracy's knowledge. In the ultra-modern shop on the High Street where excessively expensive lamps and shades were displayed behind a huge plate-glass window, Walter Bowen called excitedly to his wife to come and look, then remembered that Thelma had told him she was going up to Paddock Grange. Traffic in the spacious market square halted or pulled respectfully aside at the ambulance's summons. In the offices of Stewart, Rossdale & Dilly, Estate Agents, Valuers and Auctioneers, Mary Wayne looked down from the window of her boss's sanctum, the nose of her pretty, young face flattened against the glass. It was a window which commanded a view of the pulse of Alunbury. Being in property, the firm had naturally been able to secure the plum position for their own office premises.

Once through the market square the ambulance gathered speed. On the outskirts of the town, where it passed Tallboys

Motors, it was doing seventy miles an hour. Ned Tallboys, the owner of this prosperous business, walked across the forecourt where the row of petrol pumps stood, to watch it recede into the distance. As he turned back he raised a hand in greeting to the driver of a car that was moving past on its way into town. As the owner of an E-type Jaguar, Ned Tallboys believed in keeping on the right side of the police. Lately he had been cultivating Detective-Inspector Clay rather carefully, playing on a weakness he had noticed in that rather saturnine personality – a fascination for fast sports cars.

Detective-Inspector John Clay had pulled in to let the ambulance scream past. For a moment he had wondered whether to turn round and follow it to the hospital. As a conscientious police officer he believed that everything which happened in Alunbury concerned him personally. But he decided against it. Once at police headquarters he could find out quickly enough what had happened.

John Clay had been posted to the Chiltern Constabulary at Alunbury a bare six months earlier. It had been at his own request. Following the death of his wife he had felt that he needed to get away and make a fresh start in new surroundings. There had been no children so he had no family ties to hold him. Now, too late, he was realising what a big mistake he had made. He felt desperately lonely, cut off from his old friends and acquaintances just when he needed them most. He dreaded going back to the sparkling new flat on the Mead Estate with its contemporary style furniture. Like a fool he had sold all his old stuff, lock, stock and barrel, before moving south. Now he was wont to spend any spare time which came his way browsing round the antique shops, hunting for replicas of small articles which he cherished in his memory. Mostly, though, he took care not to have any spare time. He sought escape from his own loneliness by total dedication to his work.

Clay hardly looked his fifty-odd years. Small and compact, he carried little extra weight and had always taken care to maintain a high standard of physical fitness. He only smoked a pipe and it was rarely that he accepted a drink and then strictly whisky or red wine. When time and distance permitted he preferred to get from place to place on foot rather than by car. His features were lean and a little sharp, the nose rather pronounced and slightly crooked, the mouth usually tense and edged by a pair of vertical lines that might have started life as dimples. He wore his crisp hair fairly short and usually went hatless when off duty. His eyes were deeply recessed, steely grey and mercilessly observant. When he spoke his voice was surprisingly strong for such a small man, but he used it with restraint, speaking softly as if half ashamed of his faint Yorkshire accent.

He still felt wary of the people in this southern county. Not only their speech but their style of living was different from what he was used to. With his strict Yorkshire upbringing he could not bring himself to approve of the free and easy morals of the Home Counties, and his reserved nature recoiled from the casual affability and smooth bonhomie of the wealthier inhabitants of Alunbury. All very well it was on the surface, but half the time you felt they were laughing at you behind your back.

Clay could not quite tell why he was so sure of it, but some instinct told him that there was something vicious going on under the innocent surface of Alunbury's rural affluence. There was nothing he could put his finger on but thirty years in the police force had given him a nose for crime and he could smell it here. The whiff of some kind of big-time racket was as tangible as the stink of a dead rat under the floorboards of a millionaire's mansion.

Just about the time Inspector Clay was parking his private MG outside the police station, Geoffrey Stewart's white Aston Martin DB6 was emerging from the gates of Paddock Grange. It was a fine Georgian house of well-weathered grey stone beautifully situated on a slope which commanded a view of the curving River Speale and the parkland beyond. He had picked it up for a very good price just before the property values in the area had started to rise so startlingly.

The run into Alunbury was a mere five minutes. On the outskirts of town he slowed and pulled on to the forecourt of Tallboy's Garage, stopping the Aston Martin opposite the line of petrol pumps.

'Fill her up, Mr Stewart?' the attendant called out even before the engine was switched off.

'No, Vince. Just put in a couple.'

No point, Geoffrey thought, in leaving a car with a full tank of petrol in the garage while he was away in the south of France. He glanced towards the building behind the pumps, where a selection of high quality cars sat gleaming behind the huge plate-glass windows. Ned Tallboys specialised in the more exotic type of motor-car. He had seen Geoffrey's

Aston Martin come in and was just emerging from the door of his office.

It was hard to guess Tallboys' age. It might have been anywhere between thirty-five and forty-five. He was tall and languid. Everything about him was deliberately casual, his clothes, his manner, his voice, even his curious habit of flicking some imaginary speck off the lapel of his jacket.

'Hello, squire,' he greeted Geoffrey as he strolled towards the white car, his eyes slightly crinkled at the corners, as though he was amused by some private joke.

'Good morning Ned.' Geoffrey averted his gaze reluctantly from the dial of the pump. It was his habit to monitor carefully the amount put in by the attendant.

'How's Diana?'

'Oh, she's all right. In a bit of a tizz – always is when there's packing to be done.'

Tallboys nodded sympathetically. Though a bachelor, his look implied he understood the problems of living with a woman. 'I was going to give you a ring this morning. What time do you want me to pick you up?'

'I told you.' Geoffrey made an entry in the log-book and slipped it back into the glove pocket. 'Five o'clock. Now, no later, Ned, please! The take-off's at seven-fifteen and we have to be there a good forty minutes before that.'

'Yes, all right, squire. Don't worry, I'll be there. Seventeen hours on the dot.'

He clicked his heels with mock obsequiousness and remained standing like that while Geoffrey started his engine and accelerated away.

By a quarter to eleven Geoffrey had gone through the correspondence which his secretary had left on his desk, dictated half a dozen letters and made three phone calls. He had set on one side the matters which he intended to leave Mark Paxton to handle while he was away.

Now, with a sheet of paper in front of him, he was drafting a preliminary description of an important estate which was just coming on to the market.

Geoffrey had modernised the premises when he had bought out the ageing Mr Rossdale, but he had kept the name of the old firm for the sake of the goodwill, simply adding his own at the front. His private office was light and airy, free of the clutter that usually fills the general offices of estate agents and furnished in contemporary style. From his seat he could look out on to the Market Cross and square, past the large, silver-framed photograph of Diana which stood on the corner of his desk.

There came a knock on the door and Mark Paxton entered the room. He was looking very pleased with himself. Geoffrey laid down his pen and pushed his chair back. He picked the top letter off his pile which he had set aside for Mark's attention and came round the edge of his desk.

'Mrs Frobisher's turned down the Longton property.'

'Good heavens!' Mark said in surprise. 'I thought we were home and dry on that one.'

'Yes. So did I.'

Geoffrey put the letter down and was about to pick the next one off the pile when something about Mark's manner made him pause and look up enquiringly.

'I've got some good news, sir! This will really shake you! I've just had a call from old man Roach – he's made an offer for Lyncote Manor.'

'Lyncote Manor?' The letter in Geoffrey's hand dropped forgotten on to the desk. If Mark had brought this deal off he was a shrewder student of human nature than his employer had realised. 'What's he offered, for God's sake?'

'Thirty-five thousand.'

'Thirty-five—' Geoffrey echoed in delighted astonishment. 'Is it a firm offer?'

'Yes, I think so. I heard a rumour last week that he was interested.' Mark was talking with smooth confidence as if deals of this scale came his way every day of the week. 'There's some talk of him turning it into a hotel. He's doing very well with that place at Bridgeley.'

Geoffrey went to stand in front of the large map of Alunbury and district fixed to the wall.

'He'll want a survey, of course.'

'Yes.' Mark was smiling. 'He's asked Watling to do it.'

'Len Watling? That's a stroke of luck.'

'Yes, I thought you'd say that. We're meeting this morning – the three of us.'

'Where? At the property?'

Geoffrey turned and studied the young man's face thoughtfully. Mark forced himself to look directly into the older man's eyes, determined not to drop his own as he nearly always did.

'At twelve o'clock,' he said, nodding.

'Try and have a word with Watling first,' Geoffrey suggested. 'You can always pretend that . . .'

'I've already spoken to him. His car has broken down so I'm giving him a lift.'

'Good.' Geoffrey glanced down at his wristwatch. 'A quarter to eleven. I suppose you wouldn't like me to come along?'

'I wish you would, sir,' Mark said eagerly, his eyes on Geoffrey's hand as it picked up the unfinished draft, crumpled it into a ball and flung it into the waste-paper basket. 'I was going to suggest it. It would be a great help. You know what Bob Roach is like. He loves to be made a fuss of. You could be buttering him up while I pick up Watling.'

He waited, a little on edge and nervous. Geoffrey had slid his appointment book towards him and was studying the entries.

'Yes, all right, Mark. This draft specification will just have to wait. Give me twenty minutes to deal with the rest of this bumf and I'll be with you.'

Mark nodded again, obviously relieved that Geoffrey had made the offer. Just for an instant his glance flickered down to the photograph of Diana. Then he turned and went towards the door. Geoffrey did not look up as he smiled back from the doorway. He was scratching his fair hair, a small biro clenched in his enormous hand. Mark closed the door as carefully and quietly as if it were the sick-room of an invalid.

It was ten minutes before twelve when Mark stopped his Ford estate car in front of a pair of elaborate wrought-iron gates flanked by two gigantic stone pillars. Geoffrey opened the door and climbed out. He looked up at the sky. It had stopped raining and the clouds had lifted. There was even a chance that the sun might come out.

Mark leant across the seat towards the open door.

'I'll be back as soon as I've picked up Watling.'

'Right. I'll see you at the house. It won't take me ten minutes to walk that far.'

'You've got the keys?'

Geoffrey felt in his pocket, nodded and slammed the car door. As Mark drove jerkily away he turned towards the gates.

Walking up the long drive he was glad to be alone. The rain had stopped not long ago and water still dripped lugubriously from the leaves of the trees and shrubs which grew close to the avenue. The place had been abandoned for a long time and grass sprouted thickly on the drive. Three pigeons sitting in an elm took fright and clapped their wings as they fled from this intruder. A hundred yards ahead of him a fox crossing the road-way paused to stare at him and then proceeded unhurriedly on its way. Somewhere deeper in the wood some small animal, a baby rabbit perhaps, shrieked briefly as a hovering hawk made its kill.

Geoffrey walked slowly, shoulders hunched and hands in pockets. It was high time he took this holiday. He and Diana needed the chance to be alone together to sort out the problem of their marriage. He felt a twinge of conscience about the extent to which he'd been neglecting her lately. In the south of France he must try to make up for all that, give her a really good time. He owed that at least to her. When he came back he would delegate more of the responsibility to Mark and leave himself more time to devote to the people who mattered to him. This morning's deal showed that the young man had really found his feet.

He was still deep in thought when he emerged on to what had once been an imposing front lawn flanked by the drive, which here forked to left and to right. Now the grass was waist-high and brambles had already started to multiply.

The house itself had been built at the turn of the century at a time when turrets, castellations and mock fortifications were in vogue. Now it presented a depressing sight, the walls discoloured where water had dripped from broken guttering and many of the windows smashed by stones. It was a brave man who contemplated turning this into a hotel and reclaiming the overgrown garden.

He approached the front door, taking care not to slip on the moss-covered steps, and pushed the key into the lock. It was stiff to turn and the door protested creakily as he pushed it open. The damp coldness of the place struck him in the face as he walked in and he left the door open behind him. Fragments of broken glass crunched under his feet as he went across the vast front hall. Half a dozen doors led off it, some of them open, some of them shut. Ahead an ornamental staircase led upwards towards an ornate gallery of sculptured marble. Beyond lay the silent, brooding emptiness of the place. Somewhere, from a hole in the roof or a leaking tap, water was dripping.

Once, Geoffrey thought, as he paced towards the far end of the hall, ladies in splendid evening attire had descended this staircase to the sound of a string orchestra. He stopped. Clearly through a broken window he could hear the parish church clock in Oakfield striking midday.

Then in the silence he distinctly heard the sound of a footfall and a small object falling. It had come from behind one of the closed doors to his left. There was somebody in the house already.

On tip-toe now, he moved towards the door. He paused with his fingers on the handle, his heart beating a little faster. There had been something menacing about that furtive sound in the empty house. Maybe it was only some homeless tramp who had found a refuge here.

With a sudden movement he twisted the handle and flung the door wide open. It crashed back on its hinges, leaving a black, yawning gap. The shutters had been closed and the room was in complete darkness. Somehow Geoffrey did not want to go from the light into that darkness.

'Is anybody there?' he called, pausing on the threshold.

Geoffrey never heard the detonation that sent the echoes racing round the deserted mansion. The darkness from the room beyond had rushed out and engulfed his whole world. He twisted, his hands clawing at the woodwork of the doorway, then slithered limply to the floor.

From the drive outside the front door came the sound of a car approaching fast. It stopped in front of the steps. The ratchets rasped as the handbrake was pulled on.

Mark Paxton emerged from the darkened room, stepping over Geoffrey's body where it lay on the threshold. A dribble of smoke spilled from the barrel of the automatic which he still held in his gloved right hand. He pushed it into his pocket and moved towards the front door. He got to it just as Diana slipped in, her face white and her eyes wide with tension.

'It's all right, Diana. It's all over.'

She gave a gasping sob and flung herself into his arms.

'Now, don't worry.'

'Oh, Mark—' She put her head back and looked up into his face, her mouth trembling, her eyes filling with tears. He put his mouth to hers.

Then, still holding her close, he asked:

'You found my car all right?'

'Yes. It's there – outside the door.'

'Good.' Suddenly brisk and urgent he withdrew his arm from her waist. 'Now listen, when we've got him in the car go straight back home. Phone me at the office later. Make it about four o'clock. It'll easily be that by the time I've been to Oakfield and got rid of the car.'

'Yes, Mark,' she said obediently.

He had moved from in front of her and for the first time she saw the inert form of her husband. She gave a sudden gasp and bit her lip to stop herself crying out. Geoffrey's face was turned towards her, his eyes open and teeth bared. It was almost as if he was miming an expression of horrified astonishment.

'Mark,' she whispered. 'He looks so – You're quite sure he's dead?'

For answer Mark picked a piece of glass off the floor, polished it with the back of his gloved hand. He went to stoop over the recumbent form and held the glass an inch or two in front of the mouth. Then he held it up for her to see. It was quite unmarked by any condensation of breath.

'You say your husband only has one relative, Mrs Stewart?'

'Yes, a brother. His name is Jonathan.'

'Does he live locally?'

'No. He lives in London.'

'Do you have his address?'

'No. It's somewhere near Sloane Square, I think.'

'Perhaps you know his telephone number?'

'I'm afraid not. I haven't even met Jonathan. Geoffrey and he did not get on very well.'

'Didn't?'

'When they were young. Actually they're only stepbrothers.'

'Perhaps Mr Stewart might have a note of the address and telephone number in some notebook.'

Inspector Clay's observant eye toured the drawing room in search of one of those leather-bound books for telephone numbers which people give each other for Christmas when they can't think of anything better. He was sitting in an upright chair almost in the middle of the drawing room at Paddock Grange, his notebook open on his knee. Mark Paxton and Ned Tallboys were ensconced side by side on the settee. On the arm beside the latter was balanced a glass containing the remains of what had been whisky.

Diana was sitting, restlessly uncomfortable, in her usual chair, the one on which she had placed her mink coat some ten hours earlier. She was finding Clay's searching gaze and quiet, unemotional voice particularly disquieting and her feeling that some sort of trap was being prepared for her was not eased by the stolid figure of Detective-Sergeant Booth standing by the doorway.

'Look, Inspector.' Diana leant forward to stub her second cigarette out in the ash-tray. 'I've already told you – my husband hasn't suddenly taken it into his head to visit friends or relatives or anything like that. We were due to go away on holiday together. We were flying to the south of France this evening. Mr Tallboys was going to drive us to the airport, that's why . . .'

'Yes, yes, Mrs Stewart. I understand.' Inspector Clay firmly interrupted Diana's angry statement. 'I understand the position perfectly. But I have to remind you that the police have no responsibility towards missing adults. Your husband may have been taken ill – or be suffering from loss of memory. He might even have confused the arrangements and gone straight to the airport.'

'Then why hasn't he telephoned?' Ned Tallboys put in. 'It's seven o'clock now. The plane's due to leave in fifteen minutes.'

'Yes, of course.' Diana looked gratefully at Ned Tallboys and turned to Mark as if seeking support. 'And how do you account for Mr Paxton's story?'

'I can't account for it, madam.' There had been no need to remind Clay of the time. This call from Paddock Grange meant that he'd be eating a cold supper again. His housekeeper would never wait a minute after seven o'clock for him. With resignation he faced towards Mark Paxton. 'Perhaps you'd run over that for me again, sir – What happened at Lyncote Manor this morning.'

'Yes, of course.' Mark stood up and went to help himself from the box of cigarettes which Diana had left open on the coffee table for her visitors' benefit. He slipped a lighter from his waistcoat pocket. All his movements were relaxed and confident.

'Mr Stewart told me that Bob Roach had made an offer for Lyncote Manor and that they'd arranged to meet there at twelve o'clock. He asked me to drop him at the property and then drive over to Oakfield and pick up Len Watling. He's the surveyor, you know.'

'Yes. I know him.'

'I drove out to Lyncote Manor, dropped Mr Stewart, and then went on to Oakfield. Len Watling was out. He was in London and his secretary knew nothing about the appointment.' Mark glanced towards Clay to see whether he was noting all this down in his little book, but the inspector was simply sitting there, listening with that attentive and faintly sceptical expression. Ned Tallboys was not watching Mark but studying Clay's profile with interest and amusement. 'Naturally I was puzzled and I drove straight back to the Manor. When I got to the house there was no sign of Mr Stewart and I thought he'd either returned to the office or gone off somewhere with Mr Roach.'

'A natural assumption, sir. What time was that?'

'It must have been shortly after twelve when I got to Lyncote Manor. I waited for about twenty minutes and then gave them up. I had to be back in Alunbury for a luncheon engagement with an important client.'

Mark saw Clay make one quick jotting, and paused, waiting for some question. It did not come and he ploughed on with his story.

'It was about half past three when I got back to the office. Geoffrey had not come in. The first thing I did was telephone Roach. He said he'd never contacted Mr Stewart and he certainly wasn't interested in buying Lyncote Manor. Well, after that I just didn't know what to do. I dictated half a dozen letters, made a few phone calls and was just about to ring Mrs Stewart when she telephoned herself.'

'I was getting worried,' Diana said, taking up the story. 'It was a quarter past four and Ned was calling for us at five o'clock.'

Clay glanced towards Tallboys who simply nodded his head. His twinkling eyes were now moving from Mark to Diana.

Mark said: 'I told Mrs Stewart what had happened and she asked me if Mr Stewart's car was still in the car park. I went to see and sure enough it was there all right. Just where he'd left it.'

The scarlet telephone on Diana's desk started to ring. Clay got to his feet, folding his notebook away and putting it in his pocket.

'I think that's probably for me. May I?'

He crossed between Diana and Mark. Just for an instant, while the inspector's back was turned, their eyes met. She seemed to be reassuring him, telling him that he'd done a good job. So far everything was going exactly according to plan.

The most dangerous part had been getting the body away from Lyncote Manor. Diana had flatly refused to touch Geoffrey and Mark had been left to lug the heavy form across the floor and heave it into the back of his estate car. There he had flung an old army blanket over it, disguising its shape with a few empty cardboard cartons. He was sweating with the exertion and panting when he got behind the wheel.

Driving back to Alunbury he proceeded with unaccustomed caution. This was not the moment to be stopped for speeding or get involved in even a minor accident. It had started to rain again when he got back to the mews where he kept his car. That was a good thing because it had driven everyone indoors. There was no one about as he unlocked the garage doors and opened them wide.

He eased the estate car gingerly into the tight space, being careful to leave himself enough room on the driver's side to open the door and let himself out. As the engine died he heaved a sigh of relief, but his heart stopped as he pushed past the rear end of his car. Geoffrey's body had moved with the motion of the journey and his right hand had slipped clear of the rug. Mark could see the signet ring glistening on his finger.

He glanced to right and left before opening the tailgate. He readjusted the rug so that the body was completely concealed. He then closed and locked the tailgate. Then he pushed the garage doors shut and slid the big bolt across. Last of all, making sure that he had the key, he clicked the massive brand-new padlock and tested it with a strong pull so as to be certain it had locked. The whole job had been completed soon after one, a good six hours ago.

'Clay speaking.' The Inspector had the receiver to his ear. 'Is that you, Williams? Any news?'

As he listened, Clay's eyes wandered with apparent disinterest over the three other occupants of the room. They were all waiting with that slight embarrassment which people feel when they have to overhear someone else's conversation.

'I see. What about the hospitals? Have you checked them? . . . All right, Williams. Sar'nt Booth and I are just leaving. We'll be with you inside fifteen minutes.'

Clay replaced the receiver. Diana looked up at him.

'What was that about the hospitals?'

'It's all right, Mrs Stewart,' Clay said reassuringly. 'It's just routine. We always check the hospitals. Now, I'm going back to the station. If your husband turns up or you hear anything get in touch with us immediately. The duty sergeant will know where to find me if I'm not there at the time. Otherwise I'll phone you myself about half past ten.'

'Yes. All right, Inspector.'

'And try not to worry. There's probably a perfectly simple explanation to all this.'

Ned Tallboys had uncoiled himself from the low settee and was flicking at the lapel of his jacket. 'Are you alone in the house, Diana?'

'Yes. Mrs Houston went off this morning.'

'Would you like me to stay with you, my dear?'

'No, no, Ned, please—' Diana said, hastily dropping her pose of the abandoned little woman. 'There's no need. I shall be perfectly all right. I'll probably phone Thelma and ask her to come over for a couple of hours. I'm sure Geoffrey will ring up any minute.'

'Well, you know where I am if you want me.' As he passed her Ned paused to give her arm a friendly squeeze.

'Yes. Thank you, Ned.'

Diana stood up as her visitors filed out into the hall, smiling her gratitude in response to their encouraging farewells. In the hallway Mark, who had been offered a lift into Alunbury by Clay, made an excuse to go back and have a word with Diana alone. She had gone to the fireplace and was standing with head bowed. When she heard his step she turned quickly, her lips parted.

'Mark, you shouldn't be . . .'

'They think I've come back to give you my telephone number. Listen. I've got the key. I'll see you when I get back from Benchley Wood.'

'When are you going?' She spoke almost in a whisper.

'As soon as it's dark. I'll be back by twelve at the latest.'

'I'm worried, Mark. It's over fifteen miles to Benchley Wood. Suppose someone stops you—'

'Look, we've been into all this,' Mark said impatiently. 'Now, don't worry.'

'Yes. But why Benchley Wood? Wouldn't it be safer—?'

'Diana, I told you.' He went to her and put his hands on her arms. 'There's a gravel pit there. They start filling in a section early tomorrow morning. I've known about this for weeks. That's why I picked . . .'

He stopped, feeling her body start under his hands. Outside the window a car door had banged.

'Diana, leave this to me, darling. Believe me, once that gravel pit is filled in they'll never find him, not in a thousand years.'

She pressed herself tight against him, her eyes closed and her ear on his chest. Then, with an effort she moved away from him.

'You must go,' she whispered. 'We'll have time later – tonight—'

Out on the drive in front of the house Ned Tallboys had inserted his long form into the driver's seat of his E-type Jaguar. It was a drophead and he had the hood down. Clay was standing beside the car, running his eye covetously over its gleaming shape.

'Mr Stewart seemed perfectly normal when you saw him this morning, sir?'

'Perfectly normal. A bit irascible, but then the old boy always is.'

'How long have you known Mr and Mrs Stewart, sir?'

'Oh, I've known Geoffrey for about ten years. I met Diana about four years ago, shortly before they were married.'

'They haven't been married very long, then?'

'No. About three years, I should say.'

Clay was watching the front door of the house with interest. Sergeant Booth was coming out alone, but Mark Paxton was not with him. From here it was possible to see a portion of the drawing room but not the part in front of the fireplace.

He said casually: 'Mrs Stewart seems a very nice person.'

'Oh, she is. I'm very fond of Diana.'

'And – Mr Stewart, sir?'

Tallboys put a hand on the ignition key. 'When you sell expensive cars you've got to love everybody, Inspector.'

'Yes, I suppose so, sir,' Clay agreed, with one of his rare smiles.

He stepped back as the big engine started up and watched the wheels bite a track along the drive as Ned drove away. Turning round he saw Sergeant Booth's face creased in a knowing smile.

'Where's Mr Paxton?' he asked the sergeant sharply.

'He's coming, sir. He just popped back to have a word with Mrs Stewart. He wanted to give her his telephone number.'

At that moment Mark appeared, hurrying down the steps of the Georgian house. The three men piled into the dark blue C.I.D. enquiry car, Sergeant Booth taking the wheel. Conversation on the way back to Alunbury was confined to the weather and the state of the property market in the area. To Mark's relief, Clay had apparently lost all interest in the mystery of Geoffrey Stewart's disappearance.

The police car dropped him off in the market square. By the time he had walked to the mews where he kept his car, darkness had fallen. It was the hour when, under normal circumstances, he would have been having his evening meal but for the moment he could not face the thought of food. Till this job was done and Geoffrey's body safely dumped in the gravel pit his stomach would be tied in knots.

He had a small but powerful torch in his pocket. Opening the padlock in the dark was tricky because he needed two hands for the job and did not have one free to hold the torch. In the end he used the light of the torch to insert the key in the padlock, then put it in his pocket so that he could hold the padlock steady. The mews was deserted, as usual, and the only two windows which looked down on it were both unilluminated.

The lock opened easily with a click and he pulled the bolt back. The rear window of the estate car reflected the faint light of the night sky, with his own head and shoulders outlined darkly against it.

Better get the tailgate unlocked now, he decided, then he would not have to stop the engine at Benchley Wood in order to get the key out. Stooping, he groped for the small key-hole, but the movement was a familiar one and he soon found it. Just to make sure that this time the blanket could not slip clear of the body, he opened the tailgate up. Carefully shielding the light he directed it into the car.

The blanket had been thrown back and lay in a heap just behind the front seats. The three cartons he had used to camouflage the shape of the dead man showed up clearly in the torchlight. But apart from them the estate car was empty. Geoffrey's body was gone.

Diana was cold. She had been upstairs to fetch a cardigan, but still she felt cold. The central heating had been off since May and the electric fire did little to heat the big room. She had her pack of patience cards out and had cleared everything else off the coffee table. But she could not keep her mind on the game. The memory of what had happened that morning was too vivid. She could not erase from her mind the picture of Geoffrey's wide eyes staring at her from the doorway of that empty mansion.

She went out to the kitchen where the debris from the hasty meal she had scraped together still littered the table and the sink. Mrs Houston, who had purged the kitchen with puritanical zeal before her departure, would have a fit if she could see it now. She put the kettle on to make herself another cup of coffee and looked at the clock for the umpteenth time. Not even ten o'clock yet. Time had never passed so slowly. In half an hour that man Clay would be phoning. There was something about him which she found unnerving. He had a way of making everything you said sound wildly improbable.

The kettle wailed as the water came to a boil, startling her from her day-dream. She poured water on to the Nescafé and stirred it up.

Carrying the cup and saucer back to the drawing room she stopped in the hall. She had the funniest feeling that someone was coming quietly down the stairs behind her. She forced herself to turn slowly, half expecting to see Geoffrey's ghost stalking her. There was no one, of course, though the darkened upper floor was full of shadows. She could not bring herself to go up there until Mark arrived, and that might not be for another two hours.

In the drawing room she bent over the table, trying to focus her concentration on the cards, sipping at her coffee between moves. Still restless, she decided to take a leaf out of Geoffrey's book and strengthen it with a dram of whisky. She was at the drinks table with the bottle in her hand when the telephone shrilled. She started so violently that the cup slid off the saucer and crashed to the floor, spreading a dark stain on the light green carpet. That insistent and mechanical summons echoing from all the telephones in the house was unnerving.

It must be Inspector Clay, telephoning before his time. She hurried towards her desk and picked up the receiver.

'Hello.'

The line was live. She could hear the faint hum of the current.

'Hello,' she said again. 'Who is it?'

'Diana,' a familiar voice said. 'Can you hear me? It's Geoffrey.'

Her hand flew to her throat. 'Geoffrey!'

'Listen,' he said. 'Listen to what I'm saying.' There was a slight pause as if speaking were an effort. 'You've got to . . . identify the body. They've got to think it's . . . me. Do you understand?'

No hoax this. The voice was Geoffrey's without any shadow of doubt, but it was more like the old Geoffrey that she had once loved.

All she could say was: 'Geoffrey!'

'I'll phone you again tomorrow morning at twelve o'clock.'

He spoke the last sentence rapidly and then rang off. She was left holding the receiver, the dialling tone ringing in her ear, the room spinning round her . . .

When she opened her eyes it was to find herself lying on the settee. Mark was kneeling on the floor beside her, holding a glass of water to her lips. She started up, almost knocking it out of his hand, staring at the telephone. The receiver was back on its stand.

'I put the receiver back,' Mark explained. 'It was dangling from the desk. You were lying in a heap on the floor. What happened?'

'Oh, God, Mark! This is driving me out of my mind.'

'Drink this,' Mark said, his brow creased with anxiety. 'You'll be all right in a minute. You've had a black-out, that's all. Did Clay say something that scared you?'

'It wasn't Clay. It was Geoffrey.'

'Geoffrey? It wasn't.'

'At first I thought I was hearing things. I just couldn't believe it was Geoffrey.'

She sipped at the glass, then pushed it towards him.

'Take this. I think I'm going to faint again.'

'No you're not,' Mark said sharply. He took the glass and set it down on the coffee table. 'Tell me more about this phone call.'

'He said: "You've got to identify the body." '

'What body?'

'I don't know. He said: "They've got to think it's me." '

' "They've got to think it's me",' Mark echoed. 'Are you sure he said that, whoever it was?'

'Yes.'

'But it doesn't make sense.'

'I know. I just don't understand it.'

She pushed herself into a more upright position, swinging round to face him. The expression on her face was almost one of accusation.

'You told me Geoffrey was dead. You said you . . .'

'He is dead!' Mark straightened up and crossed the room towards the drinks table.

'How can he be dead when he telephoned me?' She glanced up at the clock. 'Not ten minutes ago.'

'Geoffrey is dead,' Mark repeated with insistence. 'Do you think I can't tell when someone's dead?'

'He didn't look very dead,' Diana said thoughtfully. 'Those eyes staring at me. All this evening I've had a funny feeling that he wasn't very far away . . .'

'You've got to get a grip on yourself, Diana.' Mark had splashed a liberal measure of whisky into one of the big glasses. 'I examined Geoffrey carefully after you had gone.'

Shaking her head to clear it she swung her legs off the settee.

'How is it you're back so early?' she demanded. 'I wasn't expecting you for another hour at least.'

He took a long pull at the whisky and came to stand at the end of the settee looking down at her.

'We've got trouble, Diana. When I went to get the estate car from the garage I found it empty. Geoffrey's body had gone.'

For several seconds they stared at each other. Diana was too stunned to speak. Then she found her voice.

'So it was Geoffrey who phoned me.'

'No.' Mark shook his head emphatically. 'Somebody took the body from my car. Somebody phoned you. But it wasn't Geoffrey. It was some bastard playing a trick on us, someone with a talent for impersonation—'

'You think I can't recognise Geoffrey's voice when I hear it?' she said coldly. 'That was no impersonation. There's something very special about Geoffrey's voice, something about the tone and quality of it. No one could fool me about that. I'm absolutely certain it was him.'

She stood up, defying Mark's incredulity. He shook his head at her over the top of his glass.

'Anyway,' she added, 'you'll soon know. You'll soon know whether I'm right or not.'

'How do you mean?'

'He's phoning again at twelve o'clock tomorrow.'

Clay was at the police station early next morning. He parked his car in the forecourt and waved a hand to the duty sergeant who was seated at his post behind the window flanking the swing doors. The usual assortment of the public were waiting at the enquiry desk. He ran briskly up the stairs to the first floor.

The C.I.D. section of Alunbury police station, Clay's own domain, was a self-contained department, approached through a door opening off the corridor leading to the various administrative offices. Those who worked beyond that door, unlike most of the other staff in the station, wore civilian clothing.

'Good morning, Alice.' Clay put his head into the office where his two typists worked. Alice was busy taking a report dictated by one of his detective constables. 'Don't get up,' Clay told the young man.

He crossed the corridor to a compact office where a rather lugubrious man with heavy jowls sat among the filing cabinets which contained the C.I.D. records.

'Good morning, Mr Jarman,' Clay used the "mister" in deference to the other man's age. 'I may be wanting any information you have on a Mr and Mrs Geoffrey Stewart of

Paddock Grange. At the moment it's simply a missing persons case but I have a feeling . . .'

'That's Mr Stewart of Stewart, Rossdale & Dilly,' Mr Jarman said at once.

Clay nodded. 'Dig out what you can on his assistant, Mark Paxton, and if there's anything on the garage owner Ned Tallboys I'd like to have it.'

'Is this a rush job?'

'No. Could be a false start but I'd like you to have it ready, just in case.'

Clay moved on to the spacious C.I.D. general office which contained desks for his four detective sergeants and ten detective constables. On the walls were notice-boards with descriptions of wanted persons, circulars from the *Police Gazette* held by bulldog clips, lists of useful addresses, a few pin-ups, a blackboard showing what duties the C.I.D. personnel were engaged on. Most of the officers were out, but when Clay appeared Sergeant Booth rose from his desk. He was a very deliberate individual, with a walrus moustache and bright blue, confiding eyes. During his uniformed days, with a helmet on his head he had been the terror of the juvenile delinquents, yet somehow in civilian clothes he seemed more like a kind of household pet. He was very thorough but inclined to be on the slow side. Clay knew that he had to explain things to Sa'rnt Booth in words of one syllable.

'Morning, Sa'rnt Booth. Anything come in on Mr Stewart?'

'No, sir. We've checked with all the London and Home Counties hospitals and circulated his description to all the Chiltern stations.'

'Mm. You've been on to Mrs Stewart?'

'She rang a few moments ago. She's heard nothing.'

'Then that's about all we can do for the moment.'

Clay went into his own office and hung his hat on one of the pegs behind the door. It was a bare cubicle which he had made no effort to humanise. There were no family photographs, no pin-up calendars here. Just a business-like notice-board showing such information as the names and addresses of local solicitors and a duty and leave roster for his C.I.D. personnel.

There were two plain tables, one for Clay and one for any assistant he might bring in to work with him. In the corner stood the inevitable steel filing cabinet. Clay's own desk was largely filled by the two multi-tiered letter-trays which stood on either side.

With a sigh of resignation he sat down to look through the pile of blue or white forms which awaited his attention, mostly crime reports or the antecedent histories of criminals who were to be brought to trial. From time to time he had to go through to the general office to check various points, and three of his men came in for fresh instructions on cases they were investigating.

All the time Clay found himself waiting. Waiting for some report to come in from the men on the beat, for a phone call from Diana Stewart, for a message on the teleprinter – he didn't quite know what. He wasn't really kidding himself that this was an ordinary M.P. case.

By ten o'clock he had had enough of desk work. With a

word to Booth to tell him where he was going, he took his hat from the peg and went out to the car pound to collect one of the C.I.D. enquiry cars. Five minutes later he was walking through the doors of Stewart, Rossdale & Dilly.

The good-looking young woman who received him in the outer vestibule attempted to put him through the usual routine. 'May I have your name, please? What was the nature of your enquiry? Have you an appointment? I'll see if Mr Paxton is free.'

Clay brushed all that aside and to her embarrassment followed on her heels as she went through the main offices to the suite where the executive's rooms were. Pretty typists stared cheekily as he swept past and young men with luxuriant hair glanced up from the papers over which they were brooding. It was all very de luxe and leisurely. Clay could not help contrasting it with the stark and realistic functionalism of his own organisation, but he was careful not to let his feelings show on his face.

'Mr Paxton,' the receptionist said, opening the door and putting a hand back to restrain Clay. 'There's a gentleman would like to . . .'

'Sorry to trouble you, Mr Paxton, but could you spare me two or three minutes, sir?'

Clay had slipped past the girl into the room, but his tone was affable. Mark had evidently only just come in. He still wore his raincoat and the pile of letters which Geoffrey's secretary had placed on his desk was untouched.

'Yes, of course, Inspector. That's all right, Mary.'

Mary Wayne withdrew, feeling that somehow she had failed in her duty to the firm. Mr Paxton had looked a little annoyed at being taken by surprise like that.

Meanwhile at Mark's invitation Clay had seated himself in the very comfortable leather-covered armchair which Mark provided for his visitors. The cushions sighed as they slowly deflated under his weight. While Mark hung his own coat up Clay's eyes made their usual rapid and comprehensive tour of the room.

It was calculated to give the impression of Paxton, the dynamic young executive: a fitted carpet, Scandinavian-style furniture, modern desk equipment, a dark wallpaper which threw into relief the startlingly modern pictures. It was evident that the occupant was a spender, who liked to be surrounded by luxury and elegance, even if he worked for a country estate agent.

'Is there any news?' Mark said over his shoulder.

'No. I'm afraid not, sir. Mrs Stewart was in touch with us this morning but she hasn't heard anything. I take it you haven't?'

'No, not a word. Absolutely nothing. I'm damned if I understand it.'

'I was passing your office and I thought I'd like to have another word with you.' Clay might have added that he also wanted to run his eye over Geoffrey Stewart's whole set-up, get the sniff of the place and have a look at Paxton on his own ground.

'I'm glad you looked in,' Mark said. He moved behind his desk and sat down. With a piece of furniture between himself and the inspector he seemed to regain some of his confidence. 'I was going to ring you myself. I'm getting worried – really worried. I'm beginning to think something has happened to him.'

'Well, it doesn't look too good, sir, I must admit.' Clay's tone was entirely friendly. 'Mr Paxton, I'll tell you what I wanted to ask you. I know Mr Stewart is supposed to be a wealthy man. He has a very nice house, apparently a flourishing business . . .'

'It is a flourishing business, Inspector. There's no apparently about it. I only wish I had a slice of it.'

'Haven't you, sir?' Clay asked. His eyebrows had risen but he did not go so far as to look meaningly round the room.

'Me?' Mark laughed. 'No, of course I haven't. I'm just an employee – the manager, if you want to give me a title. The firm isn't in financial difficulties if that's what you're thinking, Inspector.'

'Well, it just crossed my mind that perhaps . . .'

'We're making money hand over fist.' Mark was more confident now and talking with easy assurance. 'Of course Mr Stewart may have problems of his own – I wouldn't know. But I should be very surprised if they had anything to do with money.'

'Then what about sex?' Clay asked pleasantly.

'Sex?'

'Yes.'

'Well—' Caught off balance by the question, Mark was groping for words. He suddenly looked very tired, the shadows under his eyes deepening, the corners of his mouth slumping.

Clay surmised that he had not slept much the previous night. 'Well – you've met Mrs Stewart.'

'Yes, I've met her.' Clay swivelled his chair towards the window so that Paxton would not feel that he was under too close scrutiny. 'And a very charming woman too. But you know – these wealthy business men.'

'On the contrary, I know very few wealthy business men, Inspector. I don't move in such exalted circles.'

Clay smiled, as one man-of-the-world to another. 'Well, you know what I mean sir. Is there anyone else? Has he a girl-friend?'

'No – not that I know of.'

'Well, you'd know, wouldn't you, Mr Paxton?'

Clay was staring at the sky. Mark tried to see whether there was any double meaning in the question but the inspector's face was free of guile.

'What do you mean?'

'They usually ring the office – don't they, sir?'

Before Mark could comment there came a knock on the door and Mary Wayne appeared.

Mark looked up, trying not to show his relief at this opportune interruption. 'Yes. What is it, Mary?'

'There's a gentleman at reception. He says he's a police officer. He wants to have a word with Inspector Clay.'

Mary Wayne was still feeling a bit abashed at the discovery that the visitor she had treated in such cavalier fashion was a police detective.

'Ask him to come in,' Mark said, but Clay had already risen to his feet.

'No. It's all right, sir.'

Mary stood aside to let him go past, but instead of following the hurrying inspector she closed the door and came into the office.

'Excuse me, Mr Paxton, but – my sister saw a police car coming out of Paddock Grange last night and, well, I was wondering if anything was the matter.'

'Yes, something is. As you know, Mr and Mrs Stewart were due to leave for the south of France last night. Unfortunately—' Mark's eyes had been fixed thoughtfully on the closed door. Now they swung up to the girl's face. 'I'm afraid Mr Stewart's disappeared, Mary.'

'Disappeared?'

'Yes.'

'What – what do you mean?'

Mary Wayne was a very good-looking girl. In other circumstances Mark would have been quick to observe the attractive blush which had heightened her colour as she came in and the swell of her breasts as her breathing quickened.

'He's just vanished. No one seems to know where he is.'

'But – doesn't Mrs Stewart know?'

'No. I'm afraid not. No one knows.'

Mark was drumming on the surface of his desk with a paper knife. There was something unnerving about this urgent summons for Clay and he was on tenterhooks to find out the cause of it. He did not have to wait long for a few moments later the inspector was back.

He came in and pointedly held the door for Mary.

'Thank you, Mary,' Mark said, dismissing her.

She went out reluctantly and Clay closed the door behind her. When he faced Mark his expression was serious.

'We've got some bad news, sir, I'm afraid. Mr Stewart's been found.'

'Is he –?' Mark pushed his chair back but did not get to his feet. Even he had found it hard to resist Diana's macabre conviction that Geoffrey was still alive and had spoken to her. Since that moment when he had looked into his estate car and found it empty he was prepared to believe that anything was possible.

'He's dead,' Clay said flatly. 'He was murdered. Some time late last night or early this morning.'

'Good God!' Mark's tone of shock and astonishment was not feigned. At that moment he was incapable of acting, even though Clay's eyes were on his face.

The buzzer on his desk rang tentatively to indicate that a telephone call had come through for him, but he ignored it. The police must have made a mistake, but a discrepancy of twelve hours was surely rather a lot.

'I wonder if you'd do me a favour, Mr Paxton.' Clay had averted his eyes from Mark's face to look at his watch.

'Yes. Yes, certainly.'

'Would you be kind enough to pick up Mrs Stewart and bring her to Benchley Wood. We need a formal identification, though there seems little doubt—'

'Benchley Wood? Why Benchley Wood?'

'That's where the body was found – in the gravel pit.'

'The gravel pit?'

Before he could help it Mark's eyes switched to the large-scale map on the wall, a replica of the one in Geoffrey Stewart's office. He had stood in front of it while he made his plan about how to dispose of the body.

'You probably know the place, don't you, sir?' Clay enquired, watching him with interest.

Mark nodded. 'Yes,' he answered. 'I know it.'

Clay put a hand under Diana's elbow to steady her as she scrambled up from the pit where a canvas screen had been erected to conceal the body of the murdered man.

'Thank you, Mrs Stewart. I'm very sorry we had to drag you out here but under the circumstances I'm afraid it was necessary.'

'Yes,' Diana answered in a low voice. 'I understand.'

With Clay and Mark on either side of her she stumbled towards the waiting estate car. The ground here was broken and uneven where the gravelly soil had been exposed by the bulldozers and mechanical diggers. This whole area, which had once been beautiful woodland and a sanctuary for bird life, was now more like a desert. The small knot of sightseers who had gathered to watch the police at work were being kept back by a uniformed constable. Men in uniform and plain-clothes men were examining the ground all round the canvas shelter and every now and then the grey of the morning was momentarily lit by the flash of a photographer's bulb. The cars of the police officers, the police surgeon and the pathologist had been parked higgledy-piggledy close to the police van and the bulldozer whose driver had found the body. From a couple of police motor-cycles on their stands came the distorted, squiggly sound of voices talking on the police radio network.

Mark's car was the only unofficial vehicle that had been allowed on to the site. As he held the door open for her, Clay said: 'Forgive me for asking you again, Mrs Stewart, but – you are sure, quite sure, it's your husband?'

Diana's face showed the strain she was under. She had put on an old black raincoat for the journey.

'Yes. I'm sure.'

Clay looked over the top of the car at Mark.

'And you, sir?'

'Well, he's pretty badly disfigured, but—'

'He is indeed, sir.'

'But he's wearing the same clothes, the same signet ring – surely it must be Mr Stewart.'

'Inspector, I've told you. It is my husband. I know it is.'

Glancing down Clay saw that if he pushed Diana any further he would have a hysterical woman on his hands.

'Thank you, Mrs Stewart,' he said reassuringly.

'Mark, please take me home.'

She got into the car. Clay shut the door and turned to walk away. Mark was about to slip in beside Diana when he changed his mind and hurried after Clay.

'Inspector—'

Clay halted and turned. 'Yes, sir?'

'How was Mr Stewart killed?'

'Well, obviously we haven't the doctor's full report yet,

sir – but you saw the body. He was very badly beaten up. My guess is that the poor devil put up a fight and his heart gave out.'

'He wasn't shot or—'

'No. No, he wasn't shot. He was just beaten up and dumped here.'

'Why do you think he was killed, Inspector? What was the motive?'

Clay shrugged. Standing there hatless in his neat clothes with the breeze stirring his slightly greying hair he was at his most impassive. The spectacle which had so unnerved Diana and Mark apparently did not affect him in the least.

'The motive? He doesn't appear to have any money on him and his wallet's missing. If he carried one, that is.'

'Yes, he did. A very nice one. I think Mrs Stewart gave it to him.'

'Thank you, sir. I'd like to have a word with her some time to try to find out what was in it. But I won't trouble her now. I'll talk to her about it later.'

He did not move as Mark nodded and moved away. He watched while the young man climbed into the car, reversed jerkily and then drove off, the estate car bouncing on the uneven ground. The most dedicated student of human nature could not have guessed what was going on behind those calm grey eyes. He was still standing there when the estate car reached the main road and turned right towards Alunbury.

In the car the atmosphere was tense.

'I knew I was right. I knew damn well I was right! It was Geoffrey on the phone. He knew about this. He knew what was going to happen this morning. He told me to identify the body and—'

'Diana, for God's sake! Geoffrey is dead!'

'I don't think so,' Diana shook her head obstinately. 'I think you're wrong. I think you made a mistake when you examined him.'

'I didn't make a mistake,' Mark said angrily, raising his voice above the noise of the car which he was pushing up to maximum speed in third gear. 'The only bloody mistake I made—'

He bit his lip. Diana had turned her head sharply. He could see her face in the driving mirror, and wondered if she realised how very unattractive she could look at moments like this.

'Go on,' she said tensely.

He took his eyes off the road for long enough to give her a measured look. 'Diana, if we fall out, we've had it. Whatever happens now we've got to stick together. We've got to stick together and play it cool. Now for God's sake let's remember that.'

'Yes. All right, Mark.'

He changed into top as the car reached level ground. While his hand was still on the gear lever her fingers slid over his, grasping them tightly. The moment of danger had passed.

Paddock Grange seemed very empty as the estate car halted opposite the front door.

'Will you come in for a moment?' Diana suggested. 'We could both do with a drink.'

He nodded and leant forward to switch off the engine.

Diana was fumbling in her handbag for her keys as she

went up the few steps to the door. She unlocked it. Mark followed her into the hall. The heavy door closed with a thump behind them. Their heels sounded loud on the floor of the hall as they crossed towards the staircase, Diana unbuttoning the old raincoat she had put on to conceal the light summer dress.

Opposite the drawing room they paused and exchanged a glance of understanding. There was no need to say anything. Diana began to go up the stairs. Mark was about to follow when the silence of the house was broken.

'Telephone,' he said.

Diana's head whipped round. She said quickly: 'What time is it?'

Mark stretched his arm to expose his watch. 'Just gone twelve o'clock.'

Impulsively Diana began to push past him. She would have rushed into the drawing room if he had not taken hold of her arm, restraining her forcibly.

'I'll take it.'

She followed a few paces behind him as he walked into the drawing room. All the time the telephone bell continued its compelling reiterated summons.

CHAPTER II

Mark picked up the receiver and after a moment's hesitation put it to his ear.

'Hello.'

'Alunbury 8130?' It was a man's voice, but not Geoffrey's.

'Yes. Who is that?'

'That's Mr Paxton speaking isn't it? This is Ned Tallboys.'

'Oh, hello, Mr Tallboys.'

Mark shot Diana a meaning glance as he repeated the name. She moved away from him and sat down listlessly in the armchair.

'I've just had the inspector here,' Tallboys was saying. He sounded as if he had not enjoyed the experience. 'He told me about the murder – about Geoffrey. I can hardly believe it.'

'I'm afraid it's true.'

'Well, how's Diana? Is she all right? How's she taken it?'

'I've just brought her home. She's bearing up well, considering.'

'My God! What a dreadful shock for her! Look, old man, please tell her that if there's anything I can do – anything at all—'

'Thank you, Mr. Tallboys,' Mark said, greeting Tallboys' effusive offer with a certain reserve. 'I'll tell her. You say the inspector told you about this morning?'

'Yes. He called in at the garage. He's just left, as a matter of fact. He wanted a key for the car.'

The inspector, Mark thought, was a pretty fast mover. He must have been hard on their heels when they drove back to Alunbury from Benchley Wood.

'Which car?'

'Geoffrey's – the Aston. It's still in the car park, I gather.'

'Oh, yes. Yes, of course.'

'Now don't forget to let me know if there's anything I can do to help.'

'Thank you, Mr Tallboys. It's very kind of you.' Mark forced as much friendship into his tone as he could manage. 'I'll probably drop in on you if I may.'

'Yes. Do that. Please do, old boy.'

Mark put the receiver down thoughtfully, and began to move towards the drinks table. Mrs Houston's absence was apparent from the used glasses which stood along with the clean ones. Diana had not had the energy to take them out to the kitchen and wash them up. The stain from the spilled coffee cup was drying into the carpet.

'Why did you say that – about dropping in on him?'

'No particular reason. I just want to hear what the inspector told him. Diana, you look done in. Shall I mix you a drink?'

'No.' Diana ran a hand over her brow as if to smooth the worry lines from it. 'My head is splitting. I'm going to take some aspirin in a minute.'

'Well, I feel like one.'

'Go ahead and help yourself.'

He found a clean tumbler, poured in a generous measure of whisky and took the top off the ice container. All the ice had melted into water. He inserted the rim of the glass under the spout of the soda syphon and carefully pressed the lever.

'Mark,' Diana said from behind him.

'Yes?'

'That man – the man I identified as Geoffrey—'

'Well?'

'Who was he?'

'I don't know.'

'Geoffrey knew. Geoffrey knew who he was—'

'What do you mean – Geoffrey knew?'

Mark turned angrily. She got up out of the chair and faced him.

'He knew that man was going to be found this morning, that's why he telephoned and told me to identify the body.'

Controlling himself with difficulty, Mark set his glass down on the table and placed his hands on the sides of her arms. 'Now Diana, don't start this all over again. You know that Geoffrey is dead.'

'No.' She shook her head with the obstinacy of a reprimanded child.

'I tell you he's dead!' Mark almost shouted. His grip made her wince. He stared intently at her as if trying to force her by will-power to accept what he said. 'Now listen, Diana. I examined him twice. Once just after he was shot, the second time about five minutes later when I had got him in the car. He was dead, Diana. Make no mistake about it – he was dead.'

'Then what happened to him? How do you account for the fact that he disappeared?'

Mark released her and picked up his drink again.

'Somebody removed the body from my car. They must have done.'

'And the phone call?'

'I've told you. It wasn't Geoffrey. It was someone impersonating him.'

Her expression and the tight line of her mouth showed him that she remained unshaken in her conviction that the voice which she had heard on the telephone was her husband's. Just at that moment the sound of the front-door bell came from the far end of the hall.

'Who can that be?'

'I don't know,' Diana said.

'Are you expecting anyone?'

She shook her head and started towards the window embrasure. 'I'll take a peep.'

She cautiously pulled the curtain a little aside so that she could see who was standing outside the door.

'It's Thelma and her husband.'

'Thelma?'

'Thelma Bowen. You've met her. She's a friend of mine. She has a shop in Alunsbury.'

Mark hastily swallowed half of his drink.

'Didn't she arrive yesterday morning just as I was leaving?'

'That's right.'

In the hall the door-bell rang again, this time more insistently.

'Look, Mark, I don't want to see them.' Diana, determined

to make her escape, was heading for the doorway. 'I know what's happened. She's heard I haven't gone away and she's wondering—'

'You'll have to see her sooner or later,' Mark pointed out. 'You might just as well get it over.'

She hesitated, but when he saw the expression of desperation on her face he changed his mind. She had had enough for one morning.

'All right, Diana. You go upstairs.' He gave her a pat on the arm. 'I'll talk to them.'

Giving her time to reach the first-floor landing Mark went to the front door and opened it. The Bowens' faces were already alive with curiosity. They had seen the estate car and knew it did not belong to either of the Stewarts. When she saw the good-looking man who opened the door Thelma put on her best smile. She was wearing a continental-style trouser-suit today, which was a mistake for one so broad in the beam. Walter Bowen had done his best not to be put in the shade and was wearing a green corduroy belted jacket which would have looked better on a younger man. In an effort to make himself appear more trendy he had grown a carefully designed beard. He was a tubby little man, the top of whose head only reached a little above Thelma's shoulder. His comical face creased into a worldly-wide smile as he looked up at Mark.

'Mr Paxton, isn't it?' Thelma said. 'This is my husband, Walter. I don't think you've met.'

'How are you?' Mark said, taking the knobbly hand that was thrust out at him. 'I'm Geoffrey Stewart's – er – manager, you know.'

'Is Diana in?' Thelma said. 'We heard a story that Geoffrey was missing or something and they'd never got off for their holiday at all. But it doesn't seem credible.'

'I'm afraid it's more serious than that,' Mark said. Thelma was already moving in a determined way into the hall and there was little he could do to stop her. He made the best of it by saying: 'Won't you come in for a moment?'

'How do you mean more serious than that?' Thelma asked, stopping in the middle of the hall.

Rapidly Mark explained to them how the search for Geoffrey had ended with the finding of his body fifteen miles away.

'But – but when did this happen?' Thelma asked, her mouth starting to tremble.

'This morning. At least they found him this morning.'

'Where?' Walter wanted to know.

'At Benchley Wood.'

'What was he doing at Benchley Wood?'

'We don't know. No one knows. It's a complete mystery.'

Walter transferred the gaze of his beady black eyes from Mark's face to his wife's. He was nervously jingling the loose change in his trouser pocket. 'You know, I can't believe it. I just can't believe it.'

Thelma shook her head in bewilderment.

'How terrible for Diana. Where is she now?'

'She's gone upstairs to rest.' Mark tried to shepherd the visitors into the living room. 'We only got back about ten minutes ago. Mrs Stewart's taken it very well but she's terribly distressed, of course.'

'My God!' Walter agreed. 'I should think so.'

Thelma ignored Mark and started purposefully towards the staircase. 'You stay here, Walter,' she commanded. 'I'm going to see if there's anything I can do for her.'

'I don't think I'd go up, Mrs Bowen,' Mark said quickly. 'She's had a sedative and she's probably asleep by now.'

'Don't worry,' Thelma said over her shoulder as she began to climb the stairs. 'If she's asleep I shan't disturb her.'

'Leave it to Thelma, dear boy,' Walter said with a chuckle. He put a hand on Mark's shoulder to steer him into the living room. 'She knows what she's doing.'

Mark could only hope that Diana had enough wit to put on some sort of an act and would not be caught unawares by the inquisitive Thelma.

'Thelma and Diana are very close, they always have been.'

Walter strutted self-importantly into the living room, his eyes noticing everything with undisguised interest. Mark was glad he had finished his drink and put the glass back on the table.

'Yes, of course. It's just that – It's terribly difficult to know what to do. This has been quite a shock for me too, Mr Bowen.'

Walter shot a glance at him and then looked away very quickly. At some moments there was a fox-like shrewdness in those small eyes.

'I'll bet it has, dear boy. But what happened exactly. What was all this about Geoffrey disappearing?'

'Well, he did disappear. That's the extraordinary thing. He and I went to see a property together – Lyncote Manor. I left him at the house and drove over to Oakfield. I was supposed to pick up a man called Watling.'

'Len Watling? He's the surveyor?'

'That's right. Anyway to cut a long story short, I couldn't get hold of Watling and when I returned to Lyncote Manor Mr Stewart had gone.' Mark had rehearsed this version of the story so often in his mind that he was almost beginning to believe it was the truth. 'There was no sign of him. The next time I saw him was this morning – at Benchley Wood.'

Shaking his head Walter walked to the window embrasure, stared out towards the forecourt front door for a moment and then turned back. 'It's incredible. But what happened? What do you think happened?'

'It's impossible to say.' Mark felt like another drink but he was damned if he was going to offer Walter Bowen one. 'His wallet's missing. I expect he had plenty of money in it – traveller's cheques and foreign currency for his holiday abroad.'

'Is that what the police think? That someone bashed him on the head and—'

'I honestly don't know what the police think. They haven't confided in me.'

Walter halted and picked up a book that was lying on the corner of Diana's desk.

'Who's in charge of the case – Clay?'

'Yes, that's right. Inspector Clay. Do you know him?'

'I've met him,' Walter said, pursing his lips as if afraid that official secrets might escape from him. 'I know most of the local people. Through Thelma, of course.'

The book seemed to fascinate Walter. It was a cookery book with recipes by the latest TV gastronomic personality.

'Are you in business, Mr Bowen?'

'No, no, no,' Walter denied the suggestion energetically. 'God forbid. I'm a writer – a playwright really – but I churn out the odd article every now and then for the local rag. Incidentally, talking of Clay, dear boy, let me give you a tip. Whatever you do, don't underrate him.'

'Why should I do that?' Mark asked, after a short pause.

Walter did not look at him. He had the book on one side and was studying a colour photograph of a dish of dressed crab. 'You know what I mean.'

'No,' Mark said, irritated by the suggestive tone of the little man. 'I'm afraid I don't know what you mean.'

Walter put the book down and gazed out of the window.

'He gives you the impression that he doesn't know his arse from his elbow. But he does.' He paused, fingering one side of his beard appreciatively. 'Curiously enough, Thelma and I were talking about you last night, Mr Paxton.'

'About me?'

'Yes. I said you'd worked for Geoffrey about a year and she said it must be well over two by now.'

Nosey little bastard, Mark thought. He said: 'I'm afraid you were both wrong. However, since you're interested, I joined the firm three years ago.'

Walter's foxy eyes roved meaningly round the room and finally came to rest on Mark, who had unconsciously moved to the Persian rug in front of the fireplace.

'Well, I must say you've done very well for yourself.'

Mark did not feel that the statement called for any comment. The two men were facing each other across the coffee table, rather like chess players waiting for the next move, when Thelma came back into the room.

'How is she, Thelma?'

'Well, she's not too bad, I suppose, considering. But I don't honestly think the poor dear realises what's happened.'

'Was she in bed?' Mark asked, trying to read from Thelma's face what she was thinking, watching to see if she and Walter would exchange a look that might mean they knew something.

'No, she was just getting undressed. She's asked me to try and get hold of Mrs Houston.'

'Mrs Houston?'

'That's the housekeeper,' Thelma explained, her eyes resting gently on Mark. Her voice changed to a more hectoring tone when she addressed her husband. 'Walter, I'm afraid we'll have to put those friends of yours off. I couldn't cope with them – not tonight. In any case I've told Diana I'll pop back again, just to make sure she's all right.'

'Yes, of course,' Walter said obediently. 'I should stay the night with her, Thelma.'

'She doesn't want me to. Anyhow we'll see. What are your plans Mr Paxton? Could you stay here until about four o'clock?'

Mark looked at his watch and furrowed his brow as if working out just how important the business awaiting him at the office really was.

'Yes, I think so,' he said reluctantly.

'Well, I'm afraid I've got to go back to the shop and we can't very well leave her here on her own,' Thelma said.

'No, of course not, but—'

'I'll be back here by four o'clock – maybe half past three, with a bit of luck.'

'Yes, all right, Mrs Bowen,' Mark said submissively. He wondered whether it was Thelma's habit to take charge of every situation she found herself in. The best policy, he decided, was to play along with her. 'I'll stay here with her until you get back. I don't suppose Mrs Stewart would mind if I used the telephone?'

'Good God, no!'

'Don't be silly, dear boy.' Walter waved his hand magnanimously round the room. 'Make yourself at home.'

He grinned at Mark and then followed Thelma who was going towards the door. It really seemed that at long last they were leaving. Mark tried not to look too pleased at the prospect. But Thelma had not finished yet. At the doorway she stopped, struck by a sudden thought.

'Oh, before I forget. Here's Diana's cigarette case.' She opened her handbag, took out a small gold cigarette case and handed it to Mark. 'It was in her coat.'

'Her coat?'

'Yes. I took her fur coat up to London yesterday. She's having it remodelled. She left her cigarette case in it.'

'Oh, I see. I'll give it to her.'

'I'll do my best to get back by three thirty, Mr Paxton.'

Mark stood there thoughtfully, the cigarette case in his

hand. He was still wondering how much significance to place on Walter's parting shot. He heard them go along the hall, bickering about something. Then came the sound of the front door being firmly closed.

He pressed the catch of the cigarette case. It opened to reveal a neat little row of tipped cigarettes. He took one out and put it in his mouth. The light from the window glinted on the shiny inner surface of the case as he snapped it shut. Then he opened it again. He thought he had seen an inscription engraved on the inside. Yes, there it was. He held it so that the light threw the words into relief.

To Diana – who came like
a bat out of hell –
Love
Geoffrey

He closed the case and laid it on the table, went to the mantelpiece to light his cigarette with the Wedgwood lighter. It was a slim, woman's cigarette but even so he felt some relaxation of tension as he drew the smoke into his lungs.

Diana heard the front door closing. He could hear her slippers slapping across the floor of the hall. When she appeared he saw that she was wearing a silk dressing gown and not much underneath. She looked a great deal better than when she had gone upstairs and had evidently used the time to do something about her make up.

'Have they gone?'

'Yes. But Thelma's coming back.'

'When?'

'This afternoon.'

'Oh, God!' Diana sat down on the settee, shook her slippers off and tucked her bare feet up under her. 'What did she say to you?'

'She seemed upset, genuinely concerned about you, in fact.'

'Yes, she is. I'm afraid she'll be a nuisance, Mark – for a couple of weeks at any rate. We'll just have to put up with it.'

'It's not Mrs Bowen I'm worried about.'

'What do you mean?'

He sat down beside her and took her hand. Her fingers interlaced with his. She had unusually sensitive hands and their touch never failed to arouse a response in him.

'Diana, listen. We've got to be careful, both of us. We've got to be very careful. Do you understand?'

'No. I don't understand.'

'We haven't got to see too much of each other. We certainly must not be seen alone together – not if we can help it.'

He was sitting on the edge of the settee, half listening for the door-bell to ring again.

'Mark, what is it?' she asked, studying him carefully. 'You're worried.'

'No. I'm not really worried. It's just that I have a feeling – a hunch if you like – about Walter Bowen.'

'What about Walter?'

'I think he knows – about us, I mean.'

'Why do you say that?'

'Just a remark he made. It wasn't anything specific, Diana, it was just that he – Why are you smiling?'

She was pulling him towards her, wriggling her body into a cosier position. 'You had me worried for a minute. I know Walter. I know exactly what you mean. He always puts on that act – gives you the impression that he knows everything that's going on. But he's a complete phoney.'

Her hand was at the back of his head, her fingers soothingly stroking his hair.

'He may be a phoney, but . . .'

'There's no may about it. He calls himself a writer, but he hasn't written anything for years. If it wasn't for Thelma, he'd starve. Believe me, darling, Walter is the least of our worries.'

'I hope you're right,' Mark said, succumbing at last and bending to kiss her.

The kiss was a long one. A stab of pain reminded him that he had a lighted cigarette still in his hand. He disengaged himself and leaned over to stub it out on the coffee table. As he did so the gold cigarette case caught his eye.

'By the way, Thelma asked me to give you this. You left it in your coat.'

'In my coat?'

Diana made no move to take the case which Mark was proffering to her.

'Yes. Didn't she take your fur coat up to London for you?'

'Yes. She did.'

'Well—' Mark nodded towards the case.

'That's not mine. I've never seen it before.'

'Of course it's yours.' Mark threw the case on to her lap. 'It was in the coat pocket.'

'I tell you I never—' Diana picked the case up and turned

it over in her hands. 'It's a beautiful one. But it's not mine.'

'Darling, don't be stupid. It's even got your name on it.'

He took the case from her, snapped it open and read out the inscription. 'To Diana – who came like a bat out of hell – Love Geoffrey.' He handed it to her. She held it up at an angle, just as he had done, to bring the inscription into relief.

'I've never seen this case before, Mark.' Her eyes, as she studied the case, showed her complete bewilderment. 'What does it mean – "who came like a bat out of hell" '?'

Things were quiet at Tallboys' Garage. It was still the lunch hour and Vince, the forecourt attendant, was taking advantage of the lull to hose away some petrol that had overflowed from a customer's car. The weather had taken a turn for the better and the sun was shining. The public house across the road was doing good business. Dozens of cars were parked outside it and the terrace where tables had been set out under Cinzano and Martini umbrellas, continental-style, was crowded. Vince had the long-handled broom out and was vigorously sweeping the surplus water down a drain when the Ford estate car pulled in.

He leant the broom against the side of his small kiosk, wiped his hands on his overalls and went to unscrew the filler cap of the estate car.

'Full up, sir?'

'No, just a quid's worth,' the driver called.

Vince set the pump and pushed the nozzle into the tank.

'Is Mr Tallboys about?' the man in the estate car enquired.

'No. I'm afraid you just missed him, sir.'

Vince moved round to the window on the driver's side.

'You're Mr Paxton, aren't you, sir?'

'Yes. That's right.'

'Is it true, sir, what they're saying about Mr Stewart?'

'It depends what you've heard,' Mark said drily.

'Well, the police were here. Not an hour back. They were talking to Mr Tallboys, oh, for ages. Someone said that Mr Stewart was dead, that he'd been murdered.'

Vince rolled the last word round his tongue with gloomy emphasis.

'Yes, I'm afraid it's true,' Mark confirmed after a moment's hesitation. 'They found him this morning at Benchley Wood.' Tersely he changed the subject. Everybody he met wanted to talk about Geoffrey and his disappearance. It was impossible to escape from it. 'I suppose you don't know when Mr Tallboys will be back?'

'He shouldn't be long,' Vince said, his eye on the dial of the pump. The pointer was just coming round to the hundred mark. 'He just popped over to the Black Rabbit.'

'The Black Rabbit. You mean the pub?'

'That's right. He doesn't bother much about lunch. He usually has a pint of bitter.'

Ned Tallboys was not to be seen in any of the bars. Mark pushed his way through the chattering, glass-chinking throng towards the door that led out on to the terrace. He found the garage proprietor installed at a small table against the wall. Ned had draped his long form over the metal chair, tipping it back perilously against the brickwork. He had the gift of making himself look comfortable and at ease in any situation. A waitress was standing talking to him, a tray of empty glasses balanced on her hand. Ned was chatting her up, smiling at her with his mischievously amused expression.

He let his chair tilt forward when he saw Mark. 'Hello, squire!'

'I called in at the garage. Vince said you'd probably be here.'

'Yes. I usually skip lunch these days. Sit down old boy. What'll you have?'

'May I have a Scotch and soda?'

'Yes, of course. A double Scotch and soda, Beryl.'

Beryl looked a little annoyed at his interruption of her conversation. She walked away, confident that Ned's appreciative eye would not miss any detail of her performance.

'We were just talking about poor old Geoffrey,' Ned explained, his eye following Beryl until she disappeared into the saloon bar. 'She knew all about it. My God, it's amazing how news travels—'

Mark scraped the chair back and sat down. 'Especially bad news.'

'You can say that again.' Ned's pint of best bitter had hardly been touched. He wrapped his fingers round the handle and lifted it, his right elbow well out. Even beer drinking was something that Ned did with individual style. 'Tell me, how's Diana?'

'It's been a terrible shock to her, of course. Terrible. But she's a pretty tough woman.' Mark was aware of Ned's eyes studying him quizzically over the top of his tankard. He added: 'At least that's how she strikes me, at any rate.'

'Let's hope you're right. She'll have to be pretty tough from now on.'

'Why do you say that?'

Before answering, Ned put the tankard to his lips. The level of the beer rapidly subsided by about four inches.

'Well, she'll take over now, won't she? She'll run the firm, I imagine. You've got to be pretty tough in your business, squire. You must know that better than I do.'

'I see what you mean,' Mark said, a bit nettled at the other man's slightly patronising attitude.

'Still I imagine you'll be a great help to her.'

'Naturally I'll do what I can. What did the inspector have to say, Mr Tallboys?'

One of Ned's bushy eyebrows twitched at the sudden question. 'He told me about Geoffrey and then he asked me one or two questions.'

'About Mr Stewart?'

'No – mostly about myself, old boy.'

'About yourself?'

'Yes.'

'But why should he be interested in you, Mr Tallboys?'

'I don't know. But he was.' Ned held his tankard up, studying its colour against the sunlight. The day was warm enough for a misting of condensation to have formed on the outer surface of the glass. 'No, as a matter of fact that's not strictly true. I can tell you why he was curious about me. Being a bachelor I've got a bit of a reputation – quite unfounded, I assure you – and he probably thought I might have heard something.'

'About Mr Stewart?'

'Yes.'

'I don't get it. Why should you have heard something about Mr Stewart?'

'Women talk, old boy,' Ned confided darkly. 'Sometimes without realising it.'

'Oh. I see.' Mark watched Ned as he put his head back and swallowed the rest of his pint. He had been so absorbed by his own affair with Diana that it had never occurred to him to wonder whether Geoffrey might have any interest in other women.

'And – er – had you heard anything?'

'No.' Ned shook his head emphatically and set the empty tankard down with a clang on the metal table. He looked Mark straight in the eye. 'No, I hadn't. Not about Geoffrey Stewart.'

'A double Scotch and soda, wasn't it?'

Grateful for the interruption Mark turned round to find Beryl at his shoulder with a glass and a small bottle of soda water on a tray.

'Yes. That's right. Thank you.'

Beryl put the glass down and used her opener on the soda-water bottle. The top clattered to the floor and rolled under the table.

'That'll be thirty-seven pence, please.'

Ned removed his eyes from Mark's face and looked up at Beryl. The corners of his eyes crinkled into a smile again.

'Bring me another pint, please, Beryl. I'll settle up with you then.'

Mark and Diana had agreed not to see each other for the time being. He had not even thought it wise to stay at Paddock

Grange until Thelma came back. That situation seemed to have been set up too deliberately by Walter and Thelma. He could always plead that an urgent summons had called him back to the office. In fact a huge back-log of work had accumulated during the Monday and Tuesday morning. Even by Wednesday morning he was still trying desperately to catch up. He did not intend to linger in Alunbury longer than was necessary. The sooner he and Diana could get abroad on their own the better. But he had to put up a convincing show and persevere with the pretence that he was a loyal assistant doing his very best in the absence of his superior. The way things had turned out made it even more necessary, for now he had not only the police and local gossips to contend with but also the Press. The dramatic circumstances of Geoffrey Stewart's disappearance and murder had attracted the interest of the big dailies and they had sent their most ruthless bloodhounds down to dig out a story. There were photographers too, for Diana was photogenic enough to give the story an added spice.

He was working on the specification which Geoffrey had left unfinished when Mary Wayne came to his office. She was strained and harassed.

'Excuse me, Mr Paxton. Inspector Clay would like a word with you.'

Mark scooped up the telephone receiver. 'Have you switched him through?'

'No, he's here, sir. I asked him to wait in my office.'

'And he did? That's a tribute to your charm, Mary. Better ask him to come in.'

At the door Mary halted, her hand going to her mouth.

'Oh, there's something I nearly forgot. Mrs Stewart telephoned. She wanted to speak to you.'

'When was this?'

'About half an hour ago. It was while you were at the bank.'

Mark frowned. 'You should have told me.'

'Yes, I'm sorry I forgot.' Mary Wayne shook her head as if she could scarcely believe this lapse on her part. 'It's been such a busy morning, Mr Paxton. Those newspapermen haven't given me a moment's peace and I haven't known which way to turn—'

'Did Mrs Stewart say what she wanted?' Mark cut tersely into Mary's excuses.

'No. I asked her but she wouldn't tell me. She sounded very tired, poor woman.'

'Yes, I expect she did. I don't suppose she slept a wink all night. I know I didn't.' He gave her a nod of dismissal. 'All right, Mary, I'll see the inspector.'

When, a minute later, Clay was shown into the room, Mark had come out from behind his desk and was waiting with his most affable smile. He was determined to put up a better show during this interview than on the previous occasion.

'Come in, Inspector,' he said cordially. He turned to Mary. 'If Mrs Stewart phones tell her I'll ring her back later.'

'Yes, Mr Paxton.' Mary nodded her comprehension and made her exit.

'Sit down, Inspector.'

Clay was wearing a light check suit this morning. He looked very spry and well-groomed. He wore the confident expression of the dog who has two tails but does not mean to wag them yet. He sat down in the sighing leather chair and watched Mark pull forward another easy chair.

'Have you seen Mrs Stewart this morning, sir?'

'No, I haven't,' Mark said with conscious virtue. 'I haven't seen her since I brought her back from Benchley Wood yesterday. Apparently she phoned me, but I was out.'

'I was just wondering how she was, sir.' Clay was unzipping a black briefcase he had laid on his knee. 'As a matter of fact I've got some news for her. I'm hoping that it might be good news, sir.'

'Good news, Inspector?' Mark said, with an uncomfortable premonition that Clay was about to spring another of his surprises.

'Yes, sir. I'm sure you have a very busy day ahead of you, so I won't waste your time.'

Clay had produced a pair of men's driving gloves from the briefcase. He sat forward on the edge of the chair and handed them to Mark.

'I just wanted you to take a look at these gloves, sir. Have you seen them before?'

Mark took the gloves. They had mesh backs and leather palms. The leather was slightly shiny from contact with a wood-rimmed steering wheel.

'Yes, they're Mr Stewart's.'

'You're quite sure?'

'Yes. Quite sure.'

Clay nodded with satisfaction. 'They were in the glove compartment of his car. It was locked. Perhaps he'd forgotten they were there.'

'Perhaps he had,' Mark agreed, wondering what this was all about.

'They're very nice gloves, aren't they, sir?' Clay contemplated the gloves with appreciation. 'I should imagine he used them for driving.'

'Yes. He did.'

'The curious thing is – they don't fit him.'

Clay had this unnerving way of seeming quite relaxed and affable and then suddenly those piercing grey eyes would be on your face.

'What do you mean?'

'They don't fit him, Mr Paxton. Or rather, they don't fit the dead man.'

'Are you sure?'

'Quite sure. They're too large, several sizes too large. And there's another curious point. We took the dead man's fingerprints before we examined the car. Mr Stewart's car, the DB6.'

'Well?'

'We found a lot of fingerprints on the car – all shapes and sizes. But we didn't find the dead man's.'

Clay took the gloves from Mark, replaced them in his briefcase and stood up.

'Are you suggesting that the dead man wasn't Mr Stewart?'

'What do you think, sir?' Clay asked as if Mark's opinion was the most valuable thing to him in the world.

'But – Mrs Stewart identified the body!'

'Yes, I know,' Clay agreed pleasantly. 'And so did you, if it comes to that.'

'It must have been Mr Stewart.'

'Why? The face was disfigured, badly disfigured. You certainly could not have recognised him by his face.'

'No – but he was wearing Geoffrey's clothes, he had his signet ring on—'

'On the wrong finger.'

'On the wrong finger?'

'Yes, sir.'

Clay reached up to collect his hat from the peg. Mark shook his head. He stood up. It was evident that the inspector had said what he had come to say.

'Well, what does that mean exactly?'

'It means that both you and Mrs Stewart were mistaken, sir.' Clay's tone was as pleasant and friendly as ever. 'It means that Mr Stewart could, in fact, still be alive.'

He put his hat on his head, tucked his briefcase under his arm and opened the door.

'Good morning, sir. I can see myself out.'

When Diana came into Mark's office five minutes later she found him sitting behind his desk with the receiver to his ear, disconsolately listening to the ringing tone at the other end. The moment he saw her he put the telephone down and jumped up.

'Diana! I was just trying to get you.' He came round the end of the desk, but she made no move to meet him. She was wearing a dark suit and black gloves. He could see that she was tense.

'I've had the inspector here,' he said, going past her to close the door, which she had left ajar.

'I know. I met him outside. What did he want?' She was peeling off her gloves and dropping them on the chair beside her handbag.

'They've found out,' he said quietly. 'About the body, I mean. They know it's not Geoffrey's. Apparently he left—'

'Geoffrey's alive.' She made the statement in a flat unemotional tone, letting her arms fall listlessly to her sides. 'I told you, didn't I? I told you that phone call was genuine.'

She crossed the room to the window, rested her hands on the sill and stood there, staring down at the Alunbury traffic.

'What's happened now?'

'He telephoned again.'

'When?'

'This morning.'

'I don't believe it,' Mark said, after a pause.

'I tell you he telephoned,' Diana repeated with insistence.

He went to stand behind her, placing his hands on her arms, not caring if someone glanced up from the street and saw them. 'Diana, you're mistaken. You must be mistaken! Don't you realise it could not possibly—'

She twisted round, breaking his hold.

'Mark, you don't understand! It wasn't me he phoned. Not this time.'

'It – wasn't you?'

'No.'

'Then who was it?'

'Thelma.'

'He telephoned Thelma?' Mark said disbelievingly. 'When?'

'I told you. This morning. She came to the house about

an hour ago. She was in quite a state. Not like her usual self at all.'

'Hadn't you better sit down and explain to me what happened?' Mark suggested, moving her gloves and handbag from the chair to his desk. Diana opened the silver cigarette box on the desk, helped herself and accepted a light from Mark's Ronson. She sat down in the armchair, crossed her legs and leant her head back.

From the way she told her story, seeing it all over again in her own mind, Mark had no doubt that she was telling him the absolute truth.

It seemed that Diana had just finished having breakfast in bed and was talking to Mrs Houston, who had arrived back the previous evening. While they were talking they heard a car on the drive and a moment later the bell had rung. It was Thelma. Mrs Houston had done her best to fend her off but there was no stopping Thelma. She had swept into Diana's bedroom with Mrs Houston toiling helplessly up the stairs behind her.

Of course she was all apologies. 'I'm terribly sorry to burst in on you like this, Diana, but I've some absolutely staggering news for you.'

Diana managed to shut her up until Mrs Houston, whose ears were on stalks, had been shooed from the room.

'Now, Thelma, what's this all about?' Diana asked.

'Diana, that man they found at Benchley Wood – it wasn't Geoffrey!'

'How do you know?'

'You're not going to believe this. But Geoffrey's alive. He telephoned me.'

'When?'

'This morning. About an hour ago.'

'Are you absolutely sure it was Geoffrey?'

'Absolutely,' Thelma said, shaking her head with conviction. 'There's no doubt about it, Diana.'

'What's the point of him phoning you, Thelma?'

'He said if he spoke to you you'd only be more distressed and – Diana, he's in trouble. He wants to see you. He wants you to meet him this afternoon at three o'clock.'

'Where?'

'At the Pine Lodge Motel, just outside Barchester. I think he must be staying there.'

Diana had questioned Thelma closely to find out how sure she was that the voice she had heard was Geoffrey's.

'Good God, Diana I know Geoffrey's voice!' she protested. 'I know it almost as well as Walter's. I'm afraid he's in real trouble, Diana.'

'Why do you say that?'

'He asked me not to mention the phone call to anyone except you and then, just as he was ringing off he said: "Tell Diana I've forgiven her for what happened on Monday – but I'm injured and I'm in trouble, Thelma, and I've just got to see her." '

Questioned by Diana, Thelma had sworn that she had not told anyone else about the call.

'What about Walter?'

'He's in London for the day. He caught the eight fifteen.'

'Well, don't tell him about it, Thelma, please.'

'All right, Diana.'

'Do what Geoffrey says. Don't tell anyone about it.'

'All right. If that's what you want.'

'That's what I want – for the moment at any rate.'

Before Thelma left, Diana had put Mark's suggestion to her that someone might have been making a skilful impersonation of Geoffrey's voice.

'She just wouldn't hear of it, Mark,' Diana concluded. The account of Thelma's visit had lasted just about the same length of time as her cigarette. She stubbed it out in the ash-tray which Mark had placed on the arm of her chair. 'So you see, you were wrong, Mark. It *was* Geoffrey who spoke to me on Monday night, after all.'

Mark went back to his perch on the corner of the desk, one leg dangling.

'I'm sorry, but I don't believe her story.'

'You mean, you aren't prepared to believe that Geoffrey phoned her.'

'How could he phone her?' he said quietly. 'He's dead.'

Diana stood up and her voice rose in irritation. 'Mark, I told you on Monday it was Geoffrey who telephoned me. You just wouldn't believe—'

He put a hand warningly to stop her, crossed the room to the door and opened it quickly. The corridor was empty outside. He closed the door carefully.

'If you don't believe Thelma's story then how do you account for the fact that—'

'Look, Diana,' he cut in. 'It's no good asking me to account for anything, because I can't. But I still refuse to believe that it was Geoffrey who telephoned you!'

Diana listened to him, tight-lipped. 'Then you think we were mistaken – both of us.'

'Yes, I do.'

'You really believe someone impersonated his voice so perfectly—'

Aggravated by being put through a kind of third degree by someone who should have been on his side, Mark could not keep the resentment from his voice.

'Diana, I'm just as puzzled, just as mystified as you are by all this. But we've got to face facts.'

'That's precisely what you're not doing!' she flashed. 'After Geoffrey was shot, you hid the body in your car. Later, when you returned to the garage, he'd disappeared. Now surely – quite apart from the two phone calls – that proves he was still alive when you left him. That proves that he managed to—'

'To get out of a car that was locked and a garage that was padlocked on the outside?' Mark said scornfully. 'It does not prove anything of the sort!'

Diana halted in her restless pacing and faced him. 'Then what do you think happened?'

Cornered like this and forced to answer a question which in his own mind he had been avoiding since that unnerving moment on Monday night, Mark bit nervously on his fingernail.

'I've told you. I think someone went to the garage, got the padlock and the estate wagon unlocked somehow and – removed the body.'

'But who, Mark? Who would have known that there was

a body? Who would have known that it was in the car?'

The questions hung between them. Mark went behind his desk and slumped down in his chair.

'I don't know Diana. I just don't know.'

She picked up her gloves and began to wriggle her long, carefully manicured fingers into them.

'Well, I think you're wrong and that what he told Thelma was the truth. Anyway we'll soon know. If he keeps the appointment this afternoon—'

'He's not going to keep that appointment!' Mark exploded, 'and neither are you!'

'I don't see why not,' she said calmly, picking her bag up and turning towards the door.

'Diana, don't you realise this could be a trap of some kind?'

Knocking his chair back he came round the end of his desk and caught her just as she reached the door. She looked round at him with surprise and a trace of hostility.

'A trap? What kind of trap?'

'I don't know what kind of—' Mark began angrily. Then he stopped, controlling himself with a great effort. 'Diana, listen. I want you to go home and stay there until you hear from me. No, I don't want any "buts". If Geoffrey's alive then he'll contact you again. He's bound to. *If* he's alive.'

Her mood changed abruptly. She relaxed and her expression softened. She put a hand round his neck, caressed his hair with her fingers.

'All right, Mark,' she said softly. 'If you think that's the best thing to do.'

He pulled her close to him, seeing only her slightly parted lips. 'I'm sure it is, darling.'

Although he had a dozen mechanics in his employment, Ned Tallboys had a little private workshop of his own where he kept his hand in by doing small precision engineering jobs of his own. He found that it helped him to relax when things were particularly difficult, as they so often were these days in the motor trade. And besides, one way of making sure that a job was done properly was to do it yourself. Many of the modifications and additional fittings on Ned's E-type had been made in that little workshop.

He came out of the workshop with a piece of exquisitely machined steel in his hand and was turning towards the main showroom when he saw the white Morris 1100 at the petrol pump. Diana had already paid Vince and was waiting for her change.

She had engaged the gear and was just about to drive away when Ned appeared beside her.

'Hello, my dear! How nice to see you.'

'Oh, hello Ned,' she said, a little uncertainly. Just at this moment she did not want to be delayed by anybody and she knew from experience that Ned Tallboys was rather difficult to shake off.

'Did Mr Paxton give you my message?'

'Yes, thank you.'

'If there's anything I can do for you, my dear, anything at all – Now please don't hesitate to ask.'

'Thank you, Ned. It's very good of you.'

The window at her side was still wound down. She could see his face at an angle as he twisted his head to look in at her. His hand rested on the edge of the door.

'I mean it, Diana.' Diana kept her smile patiently going, but it was something of an effort. She could smell the beer on his breath. 'I'm not just saying this. Geoffrey was a very good friend of mine and I'd like to help in any way I can.'

'I'll remember that.'

'Doesn't matter what it is.' Ned's face came even closer. 'Anything to do with the house, the business, any problem at all, my dear – I'll be only too happy to help.'

To placate him she rested her hand on top of his for a second. 'You're very sweet and I appreciate it.'

He looked down at her hand on his. When she removed it he stepped back from the car. He was smiling. She re-engaged her gear and then had a sudden thought.

'Oh, Ned, you know the roads round here. How far is it to the Pine Lodge Motel?'

'The Pine Lodge? It's about fifteen miles. You can't miss it. It's on the main road just this side of Barchester.'

'Thank you, Ned,' she said and drove out on to the road.

He stood there, a tall figure that looked somehow disconsolate, watching the Morris 1100 until it disappeared round a bend in the road. Then he strolled back towards the showroom, thoughtfully flicking the invisible speck from his lapel.

As Ned Tallboys had said, you could not miss the Pine Lodge Motel. Signs had been announcing it for miles back.

The name was written in large letters over a flamboyant entrance from the main road. It was a recently completed construction standing in about four acres of freshly landscaped grounds. The residential wing extended to the right, each unit with its individual doorway and car port. To judge by the number of vehicles there the place was doing good business.

Diana turned in through the entrance and steered for the main part of the building, which was distinguishable by a miniature tower. The car park facing it was lined by the flags of a dozen nations, fluttering in the crisp breeze.

She parked her car, wondering where Geoffrey had meant her to go. Would he be waiting in the lounge or had he taken one of the residential units? Her starting point in any case would have to be the reception desk. She locked the car and started across the open space, her heart beating faster, despite the sense of unreality which had come over her. She was too absorbed with her own feelings to notice that the dark green Rover beside which she had parked was the car in which the police doctor had come to Benchley Wood the previous day. Nor was she car-conscious enough to recognise the blue Vauxhall beside the entrance as the model favoured by the Chiltern Constabulary C.I.D.

It did not escape her, however, that someone in the motel must have been taken seriously ill. An ambulance was drawn up near the entrance. Its doors were wide open. As she approached, the ambulance crew appeared from inside the motel carrying a stretcher. They cautiously descended the short flight of steps.

Diana quickened her step, not wanting to break into a run, but none the less curious to see the form on the stretcher. It was covered by a blanket, even over the face, and something about the lifeless rolling of the body told her that the ambulance had arrived too late. She waited while the doors were slammed and the vehicle drove slowly off. No wailing siren or flashing light for this passenger.

Her eyes were on the ground so that she almost bumped into the two soberly dressed men who were just coming out.

'Why, hello, Mrs Stewart!' the voice of Sergeant Booth said. 'We've just been trying to get in touch with you.'

Diana looked up with a start. Inspector Clay was at Booth's shoulder.

'What is it? What's happened?'

Inspector Clay shot Booth a quick look of warning then stepped forward. His face was serious but there was compassion in his expression as well as curiosity.

'We had an anonymous call about your husband, Mrs Stewart I'm afraid – he's dead after all.' He paused, watching her catch her breath and bite her lip so as not to cry out. 'We found the body about half an hour ago. It was hidden under a culvert at the back of the building.'

She did not know whether this extraordinary feeling she had was due to grief or relief, so it hardly mattered what Clay's sharp eyes noticed.

'What – what happened to him?'

'He was murdered, I'm afraid. Shot.'

'Shot?' Her voice was scarcely more than a whisper.

'Yes,' Clay said in his unemotional, matter of fact way.

'According to the doctor he's been dead for some time. A couple of days in fact.'

Kitty Tracy had seen the white Morris 1100 leaving Alunbury for its journey to the Pine Lodge Motel. She had just been round to the post office to lodge some money and was inserting the key into the door of her little shop in Station Road. Apart from a kitchen which had been built on at the back, the ground floor was entirely occupied by the sweet-shop. Access to the upper floor could only be gained via the staircase which went up from the back of the shop.

Kitty Tracy did not lock the door behind her, but left the hanging sign with the word CLOSED facing outside. Without removing her bird's nest hat she climbed the stairs, muttering to herself in her broad Dublin brogue. There was a small landing beyond the balustrade at the top of the stairs. Three doors opened off it. The one to the right led to Kitty's bedroom. She turned left and entered her sitting room.

The room, which was dimly lit by the small window, looked as if an unsuccessful jumble sale had been held in it. There was a dilapidated sofa, a complicated wooden framework for drying clothes in front of the gas fire, an ill-matched assortment of tables and chairs and a startlingly modern television set. The best chair in the room was occupied by a large white cat which watched Kitty with haughty, enormous eyes as she hunted for some uncluttered surface on which to put down her handbag. The only empty space she found was on top of the T.V. set.

She stood in the middle of the room, fingering the beads which hung about her neck in profusion. She carried as much intricate decoration on her person as a gypsy fortune-teller. The Victorian clock on the mantelpiece chimed half past three in husky but resonant tones. Kitty listened to it with her head cocked on one side like a bird. Then, with quick movements, she went to a table on which a telephone stood and started to dial a number.

Mark Paxton was standing behind his desk smoking a cigarette when Mary Wayne came in. She was carrying a folder full of freshly typed letters for him to sign.

'There's a Miss Tracy on the phone. She's most anxious to speak to you.'

'Tracy?'

'Yes. This is the second time she's called. She rang about half an hour ago and I said, you were out.'

'Who is she?' Mark asked, opening the folder so that he could check through the first letter. 'Do we know her?'

'She's the little Irish woman who has the sweet-shop in Station Road.'

'Oh, I know. She looks like Old Mother Riley in person. A bit dotty, I should think.'

Mary laughed. 'That's right.'

Mark sat down and picked up his pen. 'Tell her I'm engaged but find out what she wants.'

'Well, I'll try.' Mary looked doubtful. 'She's very persistent. She'll only ring back later.'

'Oh, all right. Put her on.'

Mark had checked through a couple of letters and added his signature when the phone on his desk gave one ring. He picked it up and adopted his most formal business voice.

'Mark Paxton speaking.'

'Good afternoon, Mr Paxton.' Kitty's best O'Connell Street accent came through clearly. 'I'm Kitty Tracy. We've never met but I dare say you're acquainted with my little shop in Station Road . . .'

'Yes,' Mark interrupted curtly. 'What can I do for you, Miss Tracy?'

'Well, now, I don't know that *you* can do anything for *me.* It's meself has some information for you.'

'Information? About what?'

While he was talking Mark was checking the next letter, the hand holding the pen poised ready to sign.

'About a friend of yours – Mrs Stewart.'

Mark dropped the pen on the letter and half turned in his chair.

'What about Mrs Stewart?' he asked warily. Kitty made him wait for the answer.

'She's been arrested.'

'Arrested?'

'That's right, for murder.' She pronounced the word "morther". Then, as Mark was bereft of speech she went on:

'I don't have to tell you whose murder, do I, Mr Paxton?'

'When was she arrested?'

'This afternoon.'

'Where?'

'At Pine Lodge Motel.'

He put his hand over the mouthpiece for a moment. Then, getting a hold of himself, spoke again.

'How – how do you know about this?'

'I made it my business to find out, Mr Paxton. Just as I made it my business to find out about you and Mrs Stewart.' The voice faded, as if she had turned her head away from the mouthpiece. Mark pushed a finger into the other ear as he strove to catch what she was saying. 'And that other little matter, of course.'

'What other little matter?'

'Why,' Kitty said pleasantly, her voice returning to full strength. 'The bat out of Hell—'

A click told him that the receiver had been replaced. He was left with the dialling tone burring in his ear.

CHAPTER III

The upright chair in Clay's office was far from comfortable. Diana found that the only thing to do was to sit absolutely erect, in a rather prim and proper way. It was not a position she was accustomed to and she was conscious, even in this crisis, that it did not show her off to the best advantage.

'Do you mind if I smoke?' she asked.

'Not at all,' Clay said.

He watched her whilst she searched in her handbag, found a packet of cigarettes and lit up. Clay had no means of offering her a light, but he did at least push an ash-tray towards her side of the table which separated them. The police clerk seated at the spare desk was taking advantage of the pause in Clay's questioning to catch up with his note-taking.

Strangely enough Diana had found that the interrogation had steadied her nerves. After the shock of Clay's statement at the Pine Lodge Motel she had had once again to go through the grisly business of identifying the body in the police mortuary. This time there was no room for doubt. Though Geoffrey had been dead for two days and was wearing clothes she had never seen before, his features were recognisable.

Clay had taken her back to his office. His manner had been considerate and understanding. He had given her time to compose herself, but once in the office he had left her in little doubt that there were certain questions to which he wanted an answer. In his own department of the police station, Clay was an impressively authoritative figure. She could tell by the way his subordinates treated him that, though they might not like him, they very much respected him.

'Now, let's just get this absolutely straight, Mrs Stewart. You went to the motel expecting to meet your husband?'

'Yes.'

'Though you had identified the man we found at Benchley Wood as your husband?'

'Well – to be quite honest I didn't know what to expect. Thelma – Mrs Bowen was so positive that it was Geoffrey she had heard on the phone.'

'But you must have known that to be impossible.'

'In a way I did, yes. But Thelma told me that he had sounded desperate and in need of help and I felt that – Well, I really felt that I had no alternative but to keep this appointment.'

'It did not occur to you,' Clay asked in his most sceptical tone, 'that perhaps the best thing to do was to get in touch with me?'

'No, I'm afraid it didn't. I'm sorry, Inspector, but I was so worried, so confused – I just didn't know what to do.'

'You had no one to turn to.' It was more a statement than a question.

She looked at him gratefully. 'No. No one.'

'You didn't tell anyone else about this phone call?' She hesitated for a fraction of a second. He could check her answer with Mark, but she was pretty sure she knew what Mark would say. 'No. And I asked Thelma not to mention it to anyone either – not even to her husband.'

'I see.' Clay doodled on his blotter, pursing his lips thoughtfully. 'And you knew exactly where to go? You knew where Pine Lodge Motel was?'

'No. I had to ask directions about that.'

'And whom did you ask?'

'I asked at Tallboys' garage. I had to stop there for petrol.'

'Did you ask Mr Tallboys?'

'Yes. He came over to speak to me. He's been very sympathetic since Geoffrey – since—'

'And on this occasion he was able to help you?'

'Well, he knows all the roads round these parts.'

Someone came along the corridor and knocked on the door of Clay's office. He leant forward and pressed a button which caused the "engaged" sign to light up on the wall outside. The steps receded.

'Inspector, may I ask you a few questions?'

Clay glanced up and nodded. 'Certainly. Go ahead.' His face expressed the most lively interest, as if he hoped to learn as much from Diana's questions as from his own. The clerk stopped writing, a little taken aback by this reversal of procedure.

'How did you find out about – how did you know where to find – my husband?'

'We received an anonymous letter. It arrived by the second post this morning.'

Clay slid open the drawer of his desk and extracted a plain sheet of paper which had been folded twice. He opened it out and passed it across the table to her. Diana pushed her unfinished cigarette into the ash-tray, twisting it into a bent shape. Clay's nostrils wrinkled in faint distaste.

The message was printed in block capitals in the centre of the paper. There was no address or signature.

THE BODY OF GEOFFREY STEWART
IS AT THE PINE LODGE MOTEL

'You've no idea who sent this?'

Clay, who had been reading Diana's expression as she studied the note, leant across to take it from her.

'No. I'm afraid we haven't.' He put the sheet back in the drawer and closed it. 'Not yet. As you know we found your husband's body in a ditch that runs at the back of the motel. It was covered with earth and leaves and it took us some time before we found it. According to the doctor it had been there about forty-eight hours. Since the murder was committed, in fact.'

'Then you think that happened on Monday – the day he disappeared?'

'Yes, I do,' Clay said, regarding her thoughtfully. 'I think he was shot on Monday, probably quite near the spot where Mr Paxton left him, and then taken to the motel on Monday night, when everyone was asleep.'

'But why the motel?' Diana persisted, determined to get as much out of Clay as she could. She had seen too much of him to underestimate him. He might be cold, he might be dangerous, he might have the whole edifice of the law behind him, but at least he was tangible. He almost seemed like an ally, compared with the dark and mysterious forces which she felt were lurking in the background and in whose grip she had been like a puppet ever since that terrifying phone call on Monday night. 'Why the Pine Lodge Motel? If, as you suspect, the murder was committed near Alunbury, I fail to see—'

'I can't tell you why they took him to the motel. Unless, of course—' Clay stopped at a sudden thought, then his mouth twitched with a small smile of gratitude. 'Unless that's where the switch was made.'

'The switch?'

'With the clothes. You haven't forgotten, have you, that the man we found at Benchley Wood was dressed in your husband's clothes and was wearing his signet ring?'

'Oh, yes. Of course.' Diana hollowed her spine and pressed her shoulders back, perfectly aware that the police clerk was admiring her figure in profile. Perched on this chair she felt like a little girl who has been summoned before the head-master of some co-educational school. Clay seemed completely impervious to feminine blandishments. 'Inspector, have you any idea who that man really was?'

'Yes. We identified him this morning. Does the name Harding mean anything to you, Mrs Stewart?'

'No,' Diana said, meeting the inspector's eye with complete candour. 'I don't think so. Was that his name?'

'Yes. Ken Harding. He ran a betting shop at Oakfield. But according to all accounts the shop was just a "front". Mr Harding had his finger in a number of pies.'

'Ken Harding,' she repeated the name thoughtfully, then shook her head. 'No, I'm sorry, I've never heard of him.'

'No. I didn't think you would have. Now, Mrs Stewart,

forgive my turning to a rather personal matter. But – would you describe your husband as a wealthy man?'

'He was certainly well off, but – Yes, I suppose you could call him wealthy.'

'Apart from yourself, will anyone else benefit from your husband's death – financially, I mean?'

'No. I don't think so. He made a new will about two years ago but, except for one or two small bequests, he's left everything to me.'

'What do you call small bequests?'

'Well, I believe he's left Mrs Houston, our housekeeper, a thousand pounds. She's been with him for years and Geoffrey was very fond of her.'

'I see.'

The telephone on Clay's table rang. He just stared at it and after a dozen rings it took the hint and fell silent.

'Mrs Stewart, can you think of anyone – anyone at all – who might have had a motive for committing this murder?'

Diana sensed that Clay was closing in, that the phase of affable interchanges was about to give place to a more searching interrogation. She steeled herself inwardly to beat him at his own game, to match blandness with frankness and charm.

'No. I'm afraid I haven't. To be truthful, my husband wasn't a very friendly sort of person – he found it difficult to form personal friendships. On the other hand, so far as I know, he certainly had no enemies.'

'You used the expression personal friendships, Mrs Stewart. Would you have said Mr Paxton was a personal friend?'

'Mr Paxton?'

'Yes.'

'A personal friend of Geoffrey's?'

'Of yours – or your husband's?'

'I think they got on very well,' Diana said carefully. 'It was mainly a business association. Mark – Mr Paxton's a good deal younger than Geoffrey.'

'Yes,' Clay agreed. 'About twenty years, I suppose.' He glanced towards the clerk, as if warning him to take full note of his next question and the answer to it.

'Mrs Stewart, how well do you yourself know Mr Paxton?'

Mark pulled the suitcase out from under his bed. He placed it on the bed and threw back the lid. He opened the door of his built-in wardrobe, selected a couple of suits and jackets and threw them down beside the suitcase. Then he pulled open the drawers of his compactum and began to make a hasty selection of shirts, underwear, handerchiefs and socks. Half-way through this he broke off and went into the adjoining bathroom. He began to cram razor, shaving soap, toothbrush and paste into his tartan sponge-bag. His movements were jerky and hurried and he continually kept looking at his watch.

His estate car stood outside on the driveway. Mark had a ground-floor flat in one of the new blocks which had arisen on the outskirts of Alunbury. It was a bachelor apartment consisting of entrance hall, combined dining and living room, kitchenette, bedroom and bathroom en suite. The furnishing and decoration had been planned by a friend of Mark's, who had set up as an interior decorator. Mark still wasn't quite sure whether he truly liked the effect – but that hardly mattered now.

After Kitty Tracy's call, Mary Wayne had come into the office to find him staring at the telephone with a worried and puzzled frown.

'I've typed the Bridgeley details, Mr Paxton,' she began in her brisk and competent way, 'but I shouldn't send them out yet. There's a council meeting on the twenty-third, and with a bit of luck—'

She broke off, staring at Mark in astonishment. Taking no notice of what she was saying he had risen from his chair and was collecting his hat, coat and briefcase from the cupboard behind his desk.

'I'm going out,' he told her curtly over his shoulder. 'If any-one phones, tell them I won't be back until tomorrow morning – late tomorrow morning. Eleven-thirty at the earliest.'

He marched out, leaving her standing there with a sheaf of papers she had brought still clutched in her hand.

On his way back to the flat he had gone to the mews and collected his estate car, filling up with petrol at the Ford agents, who were Ned Tallboys' principal rivals.

He was rapidly folding suits and jackets and laying them in the suitcase when he froze. The chime which sounded when his door-bell was pressed reverberated through the flat. He hurriedly gathered up the rest of the things which he had laid out on the bed and stuffed them any old how into the suitcase. He had to put his knee on the lid to get it closed. As he pushed the suitcase under the bed the chime sounded again.

He closed the wardrobe door and the drawers, went through into his sitting room and stood there, staring out into the entrance hall, debating in his mind whether to open the door or not. The unknown visitor pressed the bell button again. The sight of his estate car through the window reminded him that whoever it was could reasonably assume that he was at home.

He tip-toed into the hall and stood contemplating the door. Then came a click as the flap of the letterbox was pushed open.

'Mark!' a voice called. 'It's Diana.'

'Diana!'

He flung a glance over his shoulder, checking up in his mind whether he had left any tell-tale signs in the sitting room. Then he went and turned the knob of the Yale lock.

'Why didn't you answer the bell? I've been ringing for ages.'

She slipped past him, pulling off her gloves. He closed the door and followed her into the sitting room.

'I thought you'd been arrested.'

'Arrested?' She swung round in astonishment. 'What made you think that?'

'Someone telephoned the office and said that – What's been happening, Diana?'

'I've just been talking to Inspector Clay. I must have a drink. My throat's absolutely parched. I had to walk all the way here.'

Very much at home in Mark's flat, she went through into

the kitchen, took a tumbler from the cupboard and filled it under the cold tap. She looked strained but slightly triumphant.

'What's all this about being arrested – about a phone call?'

'First I want to know about you. Where have you been? I thought you said you were going to go home and stay there.'

She put the empty glass down on the draining-board. 'I – I didn't take your advice, Mark. I went to the motel.'

'Go on. What happened?'

'The police were there. They'd just found Geoffrey. Someone had taken him to the motel and – You were right, of course. It couldn't have been Geoffrey on the phone. He's been dead since Monday.'

'Come into the sitting room.' Mark put a hand on her arm and steered her out of the kitchenette. 'I want to know exactly what happened.'

It was a relief to sink down on Mark's comfortable sofa, kick off her shoes and tuck her feet up underneath her. She lit up a cigarette and inhaled. While he prowled restlessly about the room she told him about her journey to the Pine Lodge Motel and her subsequent interview with Clay. When she reached the point where the inspector had asked her that awkward question about how well she knew him, Mark stood stock-still behind her.

'What did you tell him?'

'Oh, I played it cool. Pretended I was only interested in you because of your usefulness to Geoffrey. It was my job as the boss's wife to make you feel welcome at the house and take an interest in you, even though I was bored to tears. I think he swallowed it. Anyway, he was very polite when we parted. The thing he seemed most interested in was who Geoffrey's solicitor was.'

'Nigel Mills?'

'Yes.'

'And that's all that happened?'

'Why, yes.' She reached a hand over her shoulder, groping for his.

'I think you've done well, Diana. Damn well, considering the circumstances. But this is quite different from what I expected.'

He gave her hand a brief squeeze, then moved round the sofa into her field of vision.

'About an hour ago a woman called Kitty Tracy telephoned me. She said you'd just been arrested and—'

'Kitty Tracy?' Diana echoed in surprise.

'Yes. Do you know her?'

'She has a shop in Station Road. It belongs to Ned Tallboys. But tell me about the phone call. What happened?'

Mark leant back against the mantelpiece which adorned a mock fireplace.

'Well – she started off by saying that she'd got some information for me. She went on to say that you'd been arrested – for the murder of Geoffrey, she implied.'

'Good God!'

'I asked her how she knew this and she said: "I make it my business to find out about things, Mr Paxton. I found out about you and Mrs Stewart, for instance – and the bat out of hell." '

'The bat out of hell? That's what's written on the cigarette case.'

Diana leant forward to reach her handbag. She found the gold cigarette case and snapped it open. Mark came to lean on the arm of the settee and they both studied the inscription again.

'To Diana – who came like a bat out of hell – Love Geoffrey,' Mark read out. 'What does it mean, Diana?'

She shook her head. 'I don't know what it means. Mark, I've told you, I've never seen this case before, not until you showed it to me.'

'It's got your name on it and it was in your coat pocket,' he pointed out.

'I know it was in my coat pocket. Mrs Houston put it there!'

'Mrs Houston?'

'Yes. I asked her about it. She said she'd found it on the floor on Monday morning just after I'd got my coat out of the wardrobe, and she thought it had dropped out of one of the pockets.' She twisted round to look up at him and emphasise her point. 'Mark, I've told you before and I'm telling you again. It's not my case!'

She had never seen him study her expression so searchingly as he did now, but after a moment he seemed to be convinced.

'All right, Diana. I believe you. Now tell me about this woman – Kitty Tracy. What do you know about her?'

She closed the cigarette case, replaced it in her handbag and then put the handbag on the settee beside her.

'I don't know anything about her – not really. Ned Tallboys

owns some property in Station Road including Kitty Tracy's sweet-shop. One night I heard him talking to Geoffrey about her. He said she was a difficult tenant, that she refused to pay her rent regularly and was always causing trouble.'

'What kind of trouble?'

'I don't know.' She reached towards a low table with a ceramic top and stubbed her cigarette out in the ash-tray, twisting it firmly to make sure it was extinguished. 'Then on another occasion, when we were all having dinner together, Thelma mentioned her. She said Miss Tracy had bought a lampshade from her that afternoon and she really thought the old girl was going round the bend. I remember Ned said: "Don't you believe it, Thelma. She's not going round the bend. She just wants you to think she is." '

'What did he mean by saying she just wants you to—'

Mark stopped dead in the middle of his question. The chime had sounded out in the hallway. They looked at each other as its tremolo note died away.

Diana said: 'Who's that?'

Mark shook his head. 'I don't know.'

'Hadn't you better answer it?'

'Yes. You go into the bedroom. I'll try to get rid of them.'

She stood up, quickly slipping her feet into her shoes. He shepherded her into the bedroom and left the door ajar so that it would look more natural. Then he walked at a deliberately slow pace towards the front door and opened it.

Inspector Clay was just straightening up. Mark wondered whether he had had an eye or an ear to the letterbox. Then he saw the evening paper in the inspector's hand. It was usually dropped on his doormat at about this time.

'Good afternoon, Mr Paxton.' Clay had put a light shower-proof coat on. His hat was set at a confident angle. His manner was that of a friendly neighbour who has just dropped in for a chat. 'Sorry to disturb you, sir, but I called at your office and they said you'd just left.'

'Yes. I'm afraid I had to leave rather early today.'

'May I come in for a moment?'

'Yes, of course.' Mark stood back, holding the door open.

'Thank you, sir.' Clay doffed his hat and handed Mark the folded newspaper. 'Your evening paper. It was on the mat.'

'Oh. Thank you.'

Mark took the paper and preceded Clay into the living room. Immediately he noticed that Diana had forgotten her handbag. It was still lying on the settee. He threw the evening paper down in such a way that it obscured the handbag. He hoped that the movement had not been too obvious. At least his body had masked the inspector's view of the settee.

He turned, forcing a hospitable smile. 'Is it too early for a drink – or can I offer you a cup of tea?'

'Nothing for me, thank you, sir.' Clay walked to the window, looked out at the estate car and then turned round. 'I don't know whether you've heard the news, Mr Paxton, but we found—'

'Yes. I have.' Mark indicated the telephone on its special table, designed to accommodate the directories in a rack at the side. 'I had to telephone Mrs Stewart about five minutes ago. She told me about this afternoon, about the motel. My God, it must have been a terrible shock for her!'

'Yes, I'm afraid it was, but she's a very remarkable woman, is Mrs Stewart.'

Clay put a hand into the pocket of his overcoat and drew out a crocodile-skin wallet. He moved away from the window towards the fireplace. That brought him directly opposite the settee. The door of Mark's bedroom, now slightly wider open than he had left it, was only a few paces to his right.

'This is really what I wanted to see you about, sir. One of my chaps found it this afternoon.'

'But that's Mr Stewart's wallet.'

'Yes, I thought you'd recognise it.' Though Mark had put a hand out, Clay made no move to pass the wallet over to him.

'Where was it found?'

'At Benchley Wood. Curiously enough not far from where we were talking yesterday afternoon, sir.'

Clay flipped the wallet open and pulled out a very slim notebook.

'I expect you've seen this before, Mr Paxton?'

'Yes. I have. He used it for telephone numbers.'

Clay was thumbing through the pages. He said: 'Amongst other things.'

'Other things?'

'Yes. He's jotted something else down.' Clay had found the page he wanted. He smoothed the spine of the notebook with his finger. 'He's written the initial T. and then various sums of money. I'd like you to take a look at this.'

Mark took the notebook. On an otherwise clean page a column of figures had been entered in pencil:

T. 100
T. 300
T. 450
T. 900

He shook his head in puzzlement. 'I'm afraid I don't know what this means, Inspector.'

'I think it's pretty obvious what it means, sir. That money was either received by Mr Stewart or paid out by him.'

'Well, my bet is it was paid out.' Mark handed the notebook back.

'Mine too, sir. Which makes me a little curious.'

'Yes – well, I'm sorry I can't help you.'

Clay replaced the notebook in the wallet, exactly as he had found it. 'I'll have a word with Mrs Stewart about it. It's just possible she might know what it means.'

He was about to put the wallet back in his pocket when he paused, his head quizzically on one side.

'Oh, you don't happen to speak Italian by any chance, do you, Mr Paxton?'

'No,' Mark replied, wondering whether there was some trap in the question. 'I'm afraid I don't.'

'Does Mrs Stewart?'

'No. At least – er – I don't think so.'

The inspector smiled faintly and put the wallet in his pocket.

'What about Mr Stewart?'

'No, I don't think he did, either. Why do you ask?'

'There's something in the wallet. Just a few words scribbled on a piece of paper. I think they're in Italian, but I'm not really sure.'

Clay apparently did not wish to pursue the matter. In fact he seemed much more interested in the interior decoration of Mark's flat.

'You've got a very nice flat here, Mr Paxton,' he said, letting his eye rove over the mock panelling, the orange carpet, the white wood furniture and the daringly colourful curtains. It came to rest on the picture above the fireplace, which consisted of two coloured lines at a subtle angle against a grey background. 'Have you been here long, sir?'

'About a year, that's all,' Mark said affably, hoping that the inspector would not want to be shown round the whole flat.

'Very pleasant.'

Clay stooped to pick his hat from the low ceramic table. He had put it down just beside the ash-tray. There was no sign that he had noticed anything as he sauntered out into the hall.

'Shall you be dropping in on Mrs Stewart this evening, Inspector?'

'No. I don't think so, sir. The poor woman's seen enough of me for one day.' He put his hat on his head, settling it carefully at the angle he preferred. 'Good afternoon, Mr Paxton.'

'Good afternoon, Inspector.'

Mark closed the door thoughtfully. When he returned to the living room Diana was standing by the settee, looking down at her handbag with the evening paper in her hand.

'Did he see it?'

'No. But he damn well might have done.'

'I'm sorry,' she said contritely. 'I suddenly remembered it while I was in the bedroom. Mark, what was that about a notebook? Was it the one Geoffrey kept in his wallet, for phone numbers?'

'Yes. He'd written something down in it. The initial T. and an entry of moneys he'd received – or paid out.'

'Who does he know whose name begins with T? If it's not Thelma it can only be—'

Mark nodded. 'I know what you're thinking, the same thing occurred to me. T. for Tracy. Diana, whether we like it or not, we've got to do something about that woman. We've got to find out what she's up to.'

Their eyes, motivated by a common thought, moved towards the telephone standing on a small table by the window. Mark was already studying Diana when she turned to him again. Ever since she had come out of the bedroom he had been watching for some sign that she had seen the suitcase under the bed or drawn some conclusion from the disordered state of his room. He was satisfied now that she had been too preoccupied by Clay's visit to think about anything else.

'Why don't you ring her?' he suggested.

'You mean – now?'

'Yes. You can pretend you're ringing from Paddock Grange. She'll never know.'

'But what am I going to say?'

'Ask her to come and see you. Don't get involved in discussing anything on the phone. It's better to have things like this out face to face.'

'Wouldn't it be better if you spoke to her?' Diana asked dubiously.

'No. She'd be too much on the defensive. She must realise that I'd have found out by now that she was lying to me.'

'Suppose she refuses to see me?'

'We'll be no worse off. You don't know till you try, do you?'

He stood up and dragged a chair over to the side of the telephone table, picked up the telephone directory and leafed through it till he found the right page.

'Here she is. Tracy, Miss Kitty. Alunbury 7432.'

He swiftly dialled the number, then pushed the instrument round and handed the receiver to her. She came hesitantly to the table and sat down on the chair, the receiver to her ear. Mark perched on the edge of the sofa a few feet away. He could just hear the ringing tone.

'Doesn't look as if she's at home,' Diana said after a minute.

'She's probably in her shop. Give her time. She may be serving a customer.'

It was a couple of minutes before a slightly breathless voice spoke in Diana's ear.

'Alunbury 7432.'

'Miss Tracy?'

'Yes. Who is that?'

'My name is Stewart. Diana Stewart.'

'Oh, yes, Mrs Stewart,' the soft Irish voice replied in a friendly, confiding tone. 'Now, what can I do for you?'

'I think you spoke to a friend of mine this afternoon – about my husband.'

'Your late husband,' Kitty Tracy corrected her quietly.

'Yes.' Diana paused, thrown off balance by this peculiar emphasis on the word "late". 'Miss Tracy, I'd like to see you. Do you think you could drop in on me some time?'

'I could. But I'd rather not if you don't mind, dearie.'

The refusal was made without any alteration in tone. In fact, Diana felt sure that Kitty Tracy was smiling to herself as she spoke.

'But if it's a chat you're wanting – just a little chat – why don't you drop in on me some time?'

Diana glanced towards Mark, but she could see that the words had been inaudible to him.

'Drop in on *you*?' she repeated. Still looking at Mark, she saw him nod.

'Yes. We can have a cosy little talk here. I don't like to leave the shop, do you see?'

'All right, Miss Tracy. When would you suggest?'

'Any time. Any time you like, dearie. What about this evening?'

'Very well, let's say this evening. Would seven o'clock suit you?'

'That'll be grand. You know my little shop, I take it?'

'Yes, I do. In Station Road, isn't it?'

'Just walk in. The sign on the door will say "closed" but

take no notice. Just walk in and come through the shop and up the stairs.'

'Thank you, Miss Tracy.'

'Thank *you,* Mrs Stewart.'

Limelight Ltd was one of the most modern shops in Alunbury. It stood out among the rather drab and conservative establishments on the High Street like a paradise bird in the middle of a row of farmyard hens. Even on a summer's evening it was ablaze with artificial light, so as to show up to the best effect the remarkably varied collection of lamps and shades on display. Thelma Bowen had channelled her tremendous, almost masculine energy into this enterprise and had succeeded in assembling one of the most representative collections of its kind outside London. There were table lamps and standard lamps, wall brackets and strip lights, coquettish French shades with demure frills, brash Scandinavian shades with ultra-modern shapes, sparkling Italian candelabra of cut glass and extremely expensive table lamps on antique bases.

With an eye on the clock, which was moving towards closing time, Thelma's assistant was carefully packing a very beautiful shade into a box, using masses of tissue paper. Margery Ellis was a plump, good-natured girl of twenty with a freckled nose and unlimited patience. She seemed blissfully unaware of the monumental row which was building up in the little office where Thelma was going through her accounts. Walter, clad today in a check jacket and cavalry twill trousers, was in his most irritating mood.

'I think it's just ridiculous!' Thelma was saying, her fleshy face quivering with indignation. 'What do we want another car for, anyway? What's the matter with the one we've got, that's what I'd like to know.'

'Of course, if you're going to be difficult.'

Walter was flitting about behind her, hoping to keep out of range of her angry eyes.

'What do you mean, difficult? It's me that's got to pay for the damn thing.'

'Yes,' Walter said, nervously straightening his flower-patterned tie. 'I thought we'd get round to that sooner or later.'

'You thought quite right. What sort of car is it, anyway?'

Walter moved behind the cover of the filing cabinet. Thelma's hand was dangerously near the glass paperweight on the desk. 'It's a – a Bentley.'

'A Bentley, for God's sake!' Thelma exploded. She flung down her pencil and spun round on the chair with such energy that the leather seat emitted a squeak.

'It's not a new one,' Walter assured her hurriedly, holding a restraining hand up. 'It's fifteen years old.'

She contemplated him from head to toe, her expression changing gradually from towering rage to despairing pity.

'Walter, that hole in your head must be getting bigger every week. Don't you realise that if people see you driving around in a Bentley they're going to think—'

She stopped, looking through the glass partition at the front entrance of the shop. Ned Tallboys had come in, wearing a short motoring coat with a fur collar. He grinned at Margery and followed her with his eyes as she walked across the shop, bearing the box in her hands. Not till she had twitched through the door of the storeroom did he turn towards Walter and Thelma.

Thelma was looking belligerent. Walter came towards him with an apologetic smile on his face.

'I'm sorry, Ned, I've changed my mind. I'm not interested.'

'What do you mean, you're not interested?' Just for once Ned's easy manner had hardened. He seemed ready to be really angry. 'Look, Walter, I could have sold that car twice this morning. That's why I asked you last night whether you were serious. You said you—'

'He is serious,' Thelma said. She had risen from her chair and was standing beside Walter, dominating him by a couple of inches. 'Have you driven the car, Walter?'

'No, not yet.'

'Well, what are we talking about? Take him for a run in it, Ned. You can't expect him to buy a car he hasn't even driven.'

A little bewildered by the sudden changes of mood between this extraordinary couple, Ned glanced from Walter's bearded countenance to Thelma's pneumatic cheeks.

'No, of course not.' He put a hand on Walter's shoulder. 'Come along, old boy. I'll bet once you've driven this machine you won't be able to resist it.'

With the smug expression of the egocentric who has, as usual, got his way, Walter started towards the door. But before he reached it a brisk figure turned in from the street and pushed open the glass door of the shop. Inspector Clay's light coat was unbuttoned and his hat was set at a jaunty angle. He showed no surprise when he saw Ned Tallboys sandwiched between Thelma and Walter Bowen.

'Hello, Inspector!' Ned exclaimed in some surprise.

'Good afternoon, sir,' Clay replied with his usual respectful affability. He took his hat off as the door swung quickly shut behind him and nodded to Walter. 'Good afternoon, sir.'

Walter's self-satisfied expression had wilted a little. He fell back to give the inspector room to come forward into the shop.

'Mrs Bowen. I wondered if you could spare me a few moments.'

Thelma's eyelids did a brief flutter, but she forced a smile. 'Yes, of course, Inspector.'

'Is there any news, Inspector?' Ned Tallboys interposed. 'About Mr Stewart, I mean.'

'Yes. I'm afraid there is, sir,' Clay answered without turning. 'We found his body this afternoon – near the Pine Lodge Motel.'

'Are you quite sure it was Geoffrey Stewart?' Ned put the question to the back of Clay's neat head.

'Yes. We're quite sure. Mrs Stewart identified him. She turned up at the motel just as we were leaving.'

Clay seemed more interested in the display of lamps and shades than in the faces of the trio who stood watching him, a little at a loss how to interpret his manner.

'But surely she identified the other man – the man you found at Benchley Wood?' Walter said.

'Yes, she did, sir.' Clay turned his gaze on Walter, who was unable to meet it and had to drop his eyes.

'But you can hardly blame Mrs Stewart for that.'

'Why not, Inspector?'

'The man at Benchley Wood had been badly beaten up. His face was unrecognisable, but he was wearing Mr Stewart's clothes. I think under the circumstances we'd have made the same mistake, sir.'

Clay was moving towards a very beautiful alabaster table lamp adorned with an orange shot silk shade. Ned said: 'Who was that man, Inspector?'

'His name was Harding, sir. Ken Harding,' Clay said, picking up the lamp to examine it. 'Have you heard of him?'

Ned shook his head, glancing at Thelma. 'No. I'm afraid I haven't.'

'Ken Harding?' Walter piped up, scratching his beard thoughtfully. 'That name's familiar. Didn't you introduce me to a man called Ken Harding about—'

'No, I didn't,' Thelma stated with positive brevity.

'But surely, Thelma – That man we met at Guildford. You remember, he was in that antique shop the afternoon I bought—'

'His name wasn't Harding. It was Belling. Tom Belling. I've known him for years.' She glanced at Clay, but his back was still towards them. He seemed very taken with the alabaster lamp. 'Look, if you're going to try that car out, Walter, you'd better get on with it.'

'Yes. Very well, Thelma,' Walter said with exaggerated obsequiousness.

'And don't buy it! Just say whether you like it or don't like it. I'll deal with Ned later.'

Ned laughed, pretending to be amused, but it was evident

that he did not care for Thelma's domineering manner. 'Just in case you didn't get the message, Inspector,' Walter called to Clay, 'it's my wife who wears the pants around here.'

To his surprise Walter found that Clay's eyes were meeting his from a gilt-framed mirror on the wall beyond him. He turned and hurried after Ned Tallboys who was already holding the door for him.

Clay turned and said pleasantly: 'Is Mr Tallboys trying to sell your husband a car?'

'Yes. A Bentley. Fifteen years old, for Pete's sake!'

'I saw it outside. It's in very good condition.'

'Yes. Well, that's more than Walter will be, if he buys it.'

Thelma was moving back towards her little office. From the store at the rear of the shop came the sound of Margery Ellis moving boxes about.

'What was it you wanted to see me about, Inspector?'

'It's about the phone call, madam. The one you had from Mr Stewart – or rather the man who called himself Mr Stewart.'

Thelma turned to face Clay squarely.

'But I didn't have a phone call. No one telephoned me. It was Mrs. Stewart who had the call.'

'Mrs Stewart?' Just for once Clay was halted in his tracks.

'Yes.'

'Would you mind telling me exactly what did happen this morning, Mrs Bowen?'

'Well—' Thelma hesitated, her face showing how unhappy she was about this situation. 'Do I have to tell you, Inspector?'

'No, you don't *have* to, madam,' Clay assured her in his smoothest tone. 'You don't have to tell me anything if you don't want to.'

'No, it's not that. It isn't that I don't want to help you.' Thelma shook her head and sat down on the chair in front of her desk. Clay watched her fingers as they began to fiddle with the pages of the invoice book on which she had been working. The large amethyst ring on her second finger glittered in the light of the desk lamp. 'It's just that – Well, Mrs Stewart's an old friend of mine. We've known each other for a very long time and I promised her that I wouldn't say—'

'I think the circumstances have changed somewhat, haven't they, Mrs Bowen?' Clay cut in, quietly but firmly.

'Yes. I suppose they have.' She looked up at him thoughtfully, debating in her mind whether to speak or not. 'Well – this morning after breakfast I had a row with Walter, my husband. It was a silly little row, but when it happens, which is rather frequently these days, I'm afraid, I usually rush round to Diana's to let off steam. Well, as I said, it happened this morning. But when I arrived at Diana's I found she was in a far worse state than I was.'

Thelma closed the invoice book, opened a drawer in her desk and placed the book inside it. Clay was standing listening, one elbow resting on the filing cabinet.

'Go on, Mrs Bowen.'

'She said she'd just had a phone call from Geoffrey, her husband.' Thelma spoke flatly, her eyes fixed to the wall in front of her. 'He'd apparently told her he was in trouble, serious trouble, and that he wanted to see her this afternoon at the Pine Lodge Motel. Diana said she didn't know what to do. She said that her instinct told her that after what had happened at Benchley Wood she ought to go to the police, and yet – Well, to cut a long story short, she finally made up her mind to keep the appointment and she asked me to say nothing about the phone call to anyone – not even to Walter.'

'I see.' Clay paused, seeing Margery Ellis come out of the storeroom. She had a raincoat on and a scarf over her head. She glanced towards the office with a look of enquiry and Thelma waved a hand to her to show that she was cleared to run off home.

'Mrs Bowen, I take it that there was no doubt in Mrs Stewart's mind that it was her husband who phoned?'

'No doubt at all. She was convinced of it.' Thelma turned round, her usually confident face puckered by uncertainty. 'And that's what I don't understand. Because we now know it couldn't have been Geoffrey.'

Clay had replaced his hat on his head and was beginning to button up his coat. A glance towards the street had shown him that the rain forecast for the evening had begun to fall. 'We do indeed. Well, thank you, Mrs Bowen. You've been very helpful.'

He had already started to move towards the street. Thelma rose hurriedly from her chair and went after him.

'Inspector, wait a minute. What made you think it was me who received that phone call?'

'Oh, something Mrs Stewart said,' Clay told her with uncharacteristic vagueness. 'But obviously I got hold of the wrong end of the stick.'

Thelma had managed to come abreast of Clay. She touched his arm, making him stop and turn to face her. 'What did Mrs Stewart say?'

Clay drew a slow breath and held it thoughtfully. 'She told me that you had received a phone call and that Mr Stewart – or the man pretending to be Mr Stewart – had asked you to deliver a message to her.'

'Asking her to meet him at the motel?'

Clay nodded.

'But that's not true!' Thelma exclaimed, her fingers tightening on his forearm. '*I* didn't receive that phone call. Diana did. Why on earth should she lie to you about a thing like that?'

Clay had had to park his C.I.D. car a little way down the street. The empty space in front of Limelight Ltd had been entirely taken up by the massive Bentley which had attracted Walter Bowen's fancy. Clay slid behind the wheel and eased the Vauxhall out into the evening traffic of the High Street. It was closing time and all up and down the street shopkeepers were shepherding the last of their customers out, pulling down the blinds on their doors and locking up. The shower had come at just the wrong moment, but rather than dally for even a second, women and men were running through the rain, keeping under the shelter of the overhanging eaves or huddling in groups at the bus shelters.

Clay drove slowly to the police station and parked in the reserved space in front of the main entrance. He waved to the duty sergeant seated at his desk just inside the window flanking the entrance. The usual queue was waiting at the enquiry desk whilst the officer on duty politely dealt with their queries. Clay pushed a way between two long-haired young men in grubby jeans and went into the public enquiry office to park his pocket radio set in the rack. It would be charged up overnight ready for use the next day.

He paid a quick call to the teleprinter room to see whether anything had come in from the neighbouring divisions on Ken Harding. It hadn't. As the collating office was next door he popped his head in to see whether any messages had been received from the men on the beat which might have a bearing on his case. He had an uneasy feeling that the killer he was hunting had not finished yet. Events were speeding up, getting ahead of him. Despite the bland and easy manner which he adopted when pursuing his enquiries, Clay was aware of a pressing sense of urgency. But the day's tally of reports consisted of the usual hotch-potch of juvenile delinquency, traffic offences, forcible entry, assault and shop-lifting.

Up in the C.I.D. main office half a dozen of his men were working at their desks. Clay signalled them to stay where they were as they began to get to their feet.

'Dawson back yet?' he asked Sergeant Williams, who was studying a clip-full of fresh reports on the notice-board.

'He's waiting in your office,' Williams said. Clay pushed open his office door. Detective Constable Dawson started and nearly let the chair slip from under him. He had evidently been waiting for some time and had gone into a day-dream, staring out of the window at the fading evening light, with the chair tipped back. Its two front legs hit the ground with a bang as he jumped up.

'Sorry, sir. I didn't hear you come in.'

Clay did not comment. He took off his hat and coat and hung them on the peg behind the door, knowing that Dawson was watching him in stiff embarrassment, wondering whether he was on the mat again for some neglect of duty.

'Now, Dawson,' Clay said, turning. 'You speak Italian, don't you?'

Dawson showed an uneven set of teeth in a broad grin. Perhaps he was remembering the last time he had practised his Italian – on a pretty foreign tourist whose car had broken down and who had been so very grateful for Dawson's help. 'Well – a little bit, sir.'

Clay took Geoffrey Stewart's wallet from an inside pocket, opened it and extracted a folded piece of notepaper on which a few words were typewritten.

'Can you tell me what this means, Dawson? Can you translate it for me?'

Dawson took the paper and frowned over it for a few seconds.

'Is it Italian?' Clay asked, after a few moments of silence.

'Oh, yes,' Dawson said, with a wry laugh. 'It's Italian, all right. But it's not easy to translate. Where does this come from exactly?'

'It's just a note.' Clay shrugged. 'It was in this wallet of Stewart's. Do you know what it means?'

Dawson mouthed the Italian words to himself, scratching the side of his head. 'Well, it simply says: "You came into my life like – like—"' He paused, searching for the right phrase.

'Well, very quickly.'

'You came into my life very quickly,' Clay repeated.

'No. It's not quite that.' Dawson studied the note again. 'You came into my life like – Something that moves fast.'

The detective constable screwed his face up, snapping his fingers with the effort to find the expression he wanted.

Suddenly Clay said: 'Like a bat out of hell?' Immediately Dawson's face cleared. He laughed with amusement and relief. 'That's right, sir. That's it! That's it, exactly. Like a bat out of hell.'

Clay too was smiling as he took the note from Dawson, folded it carefully and replaced it in the wallet.

Diana swung her Morris 1100 into Station Road just a few minutes after seven. She glanced in her mirror and saw with some relief that the Ford which had been following on her tail for the last quarter of a mile had continued straight on. She had an uncomfortably strong feeling that she was being observed and followed, that she was acting according to some unseen person's prearranged plan and walking into a trap. All along she had been against going to this rendezvous. It was Mark who should have been doing this, but he had kept on insisting that it was best for her to talk to Kitty Tracy.

Mark had changed in some way which she could not quite put her finger on. And why had she felt that there was something wrong about his bedroom? At the time, standing holding her breath behind the door, she had not thought much about it. She had been straining her ears to hear what Clay said, listening for some sound which would indicate that he was about to enter the room and discover her there. Too late she had remembered about her handbag and had no way of knowing that Mark had acted quickly enough to conceal it.

He had been so certain that their plan was watertight, could not fail to succeed. Yet almost at the outset it had seemed to go wrong. She had sensed it from that terrible moment when Geoffrey's supposedly dead eyes had stared back at her with such vivid accusation.

And the voice on the telephone! She still shivered when she thought of it. That it had been Geoffrey's was as certain as that she was sitting in this car, slowing down as she approached Kitty's shop. There simply was not any room for doubt. Yet how could the police doctor have made such a mistake about the time of his death? And when she had made that second identification her one horrified glance had seemed to confirm that Geoffrey had been dead for some time then.

Gould ghosts telephone? Was this going to be the price she had to pay for consenting to her husband's murder? Was she condemned now to wonder, every time she went to answer the phone, whether she would hear that same voice again.

'Diana? This is Geoffrey . . .'

She pulled in at the kerb, cut off the engine and sat there, hesitating. Even with Mark she had been reluctant to declare her deepest fears. In any case it was when she was alone, as now, that they pressed in on her most threateningly. At such times she felt that the two of them were like children who had ventured into a jungle. It was as if, by committing the one act of murder, they had awakened these sleeping denizens of a dark world. Why had she ever allowed herself to be involved in this waking nightmare?

A few paces away she could see the door of Kitty Tracy's dark and deserted shop. Four hundred yards back down the road was police headquarters. She had only to restart the engine, make a U-turn and in five minutes she would be in the well-lit bustling police station. It was not the first time that she had had this temptation to run to Inspector Clay and pour out the whole story, to him. He was so calm and confident, with his strange gift of appearing to divine the truth behind the lies he was told. Those steady grey eyes were almost hypnotic. She had to keep reminding herself that of all enemies he was the most dangerous.

Bracing herself she opened the door and stepped out into the road. She was about to stoop down to lock the car when she changed her mind and dropped the keys into her raincoat pocket. She had chosen a moment when the street was almost empty. A post office van was stopped a hundred yards further on and the driver was hunched in front of a letter-box, scooping mail into his sack. A man and a girl were coming arm in arm along the street from behind her, but they were moving slowly and totally absorbed in each other. She half ran, half walked to the front of Kitty Tracy's shop.

The blind behind the glass of the little doorway was pulled down, and as Kitty had predicted, a card with the word CLOSED hung just inside. She turned the handle, slipped into the shop and shut the door behind her.

'Miss Tracy?'

She had hardly dared to speak above a whisper. No one replied. The place was very gloomy and the remnants of daylight scarcely penetrated past the dusty rows of chocolate boxes and sweet jars in the window. Diana peered towards the counter but there was no sign of the owner behind it.

She moved forward into the shop. From somewhere near at hand came a faint and regular sound which might have been stifled breathing. There was a brass bell on the counter, the kind that you strike with the palm of your hand. She went to the counter and struck the knob once. The resonant, musical reverberation sounded very loud in the small shop.

'Miss Tracy?'

This time her call was stronger. Anyone waiting upstairs must surely have heard her. The row of sweet bottles on the shelves glinted back at her dully. Under a glass-topped tray on the counter the brightly coloured wrappings of Crunchies, Mars Bars and Cadbury's Milk Tray lay waiting for sticky children's fingers.

Her eyes were becoming more used to the darkness. She could see now where the flight of stairs led up from the back of the shop. Perhaps she was expected to go on up and knock on the door of Kitty Tracy's apartment?

She moved to the foot of the stairs and as she did so her foot touched a hard object lying on the ground. She looked down. It was a bone-handled flick-knife with a tapering blade. The blade was stained with a dark, moist substance which glistened dully. Quickly she stooped and was reaching for the knife when she froze. Of course, the wetness must be blood. From her crouching position she could see the staircase, which was illuminated by a skylight window in the ceiling. Just at the top of the flight of steps and partially concealed by the ornate Victorian banisters a motionless figure lay slumped. One hand had come thrusting through the banisters and hung limply down. Even without the large amethyst ring on the second finger, Diana recognised the very distinctive hand of Thelma Bowen.

'I wish to God you'd worn gloves.'

'I just didn't think about it. Why should I? I didn't know what I was walking into.'

'But you're sure, quite sure that you didn't touch the knife?'

'Yes.'

'You sound doubtful about it.'

'Well, I don't think I touched it. I—'

'You don't think? Diana, for God's sake! This is important. If you left your fingerprints on that bloody knife then ten to one—'

'I didn't touch it,' Diana broke in tensely. 'I've just told you I didn't touch it!'

It had been almost dark when Diana had got back to Paddock Grange. She had very little memory of how she had got her car started, nor of the drive back home. Mercifully Mark, whom she had arranged to meet at Paddock Grange after her visit to Kitty Tracy, was already there. He had quieted her mounting hysteria, poured her a stiff whisky and made her sit down on the settee with her legs up.

Now he reached down to take the still unfinished glass from her shaking hand, carried it over to the drinks table and set it down there. For a moment he stood, staring at the back of her head, a strange expression on his face. Then he came back and perched on the arm of a chair, facing her. She looked up at him with defensive resentment, biting her lips. Her face was very pale and her eyes still had a hunted look.

Mark spoke more quietly. 'Now tell me again what happened.'

'I've told you twice already.'

'Tell me again,' he said, with an obvious effort to control his impatience.

'When I walked into the shop, I found—'

'No. Start at the very beginning. You drove up in the car.'

'Yes. I parked it about twenty yards from the shop. There was hardly anybody about.'

'You mean the street was deserted?'

'Well, not quite. There was a post office van quite a long way off and a courting couple coming along the pavement. But I'm sure they didn't notice me.'

Mark groaned. 'You're sure of that?'

'Yes. I'm sure. When I arrived at the shop there was a CLOSED sign on the door—'

'She said there would be.'

'I took no notice of it and walked straight in.'

'Did the bell ring?'

'I didn't ring the bell. At least—'

'No, the bell above the door. The shop bell.'

'No. It didn't ring, now you come to mention it.'

She paused, gazing unseeingly at him, casting her thoughts back.

'Go on.'

'The shop was empty. I stood for a moment wondering what to do, then I noticed a bell on the counter – one of those old-fashioned little bells. I rang it and called her name. Nothing happened. It had seemed very dark at first but my eyes were becoming accustomed to the gloom. I went towards the staircase at the back of the shop and that was when I saw the knife. It was on the floor, near the bottom step.'

She swung her legs to the ground and rubbed a hand across her brow to try to alleviate the sudden splitting pain in her head.

'And then?' Mark prompted.

'I was just stooping to pick it up when I realised that there was blood on it. Then I looked up the stairs and saw her lying there with one hand dangling through the banisters.'

'Did you go up the stairs?'

'I started to—'

'How far up?'

'About three-quarters of the way I suppose. I just wanted to be sure it really was Thelma. It was pretty obvious that she'd been—My God, I was frightened, Mark. I knew immediately that she was dead and I just couldn't get out of that place quick enough.'

Diana shook her head hopelessly. 'You don't realise what it was like, Mark. I thought the murderer might still be there, watching me. I just didn't think whether there was something I ought to do. I just knew I had to get out.'

Mark stood up and bent to take a cigarette from the box. 'Did anyone see you leave the shop?'

'No. This time the street was really deserted. I was

sufficiently in possession of my wits to notice that.'

Mark lit his cigarette and took a few quick puffs.

'Now, Diana, listen. I know you touched the door-knob when you entered the shop, and you touched the bell on the counter, but when you were climbing the staircase did you have your hand on—'

He broke off. The door had opened and Mrs Houston's pale and disapproving face was in the crack. Diana swung round in her seat, frowning.

'What is it, Mrs Houston?'

'It's the inspector.'

Diana stood up, shooting a quick glance of alarm at Mark.

'Inspector Clay?'

'Yes. He said he'd like to have a word with you, madam, if it's possible.'

'Did you tell him I was in?'

'Yes,' Mrs Houston said. 'I'm rather afraid I did.'

Mark said: 'I didn't hear the bell, Mrs Houston.'

'No, sir. I happened to be in the hall and I saw him coming up the drive.'

'Oh. I see.' Mark schooled his features and turned towards Diana. 'I think you ought to see him, Mrs Stewart.'

'Yes, all right,' Diana agreed reluctantly. She nodded to the housekeeper. 'Ask him to come in.'

Mrs Houston gave Mark a parting smile of triumph and went out.

Diana stared about her as if she was looking for some way of escape. 'You know what's happened!' she whispered tensely. 'They've found Thelma! They've found her and they—'

Mark stepped towards her quickly and seized her arm. He spoke softly but with insistence. 'Be quiet, Diana. Let me do the talking.'

She stared back at him wildly, then under the influence of his eyes she slowly relaxed. When he saw that she was under control he released his grip. She went to the mirror above the fireplace and began to pat her hair into place. When, a moment later, Clay appeared in the doorway, she and Mark were standing several yards apart.

'Good evening, Mrs Stewart,' Clay said with his usual affability. He had left his coat and hat in the hall. 'Good evening, sir.'

It had been no great surprise to Clay when he had seen Mark Paxton's car parked outside Paddock Grange. That something was going on between Geoffrey Stewart's widow and his junior partner had been obvious to him from the very outset. There was motive enough for murder there without going any further. Yet he could not bring himself to believe that this ingenuous and transparent couple could have been responsible for the double murder he was investigating and the quite extraordinary series of contradictory facts which surrounded the whole business. Everything about the manner and behaviour of Diana Stewart and Mark Paxton proclaimed to an observer as keen as Clay that they had guilty consciences, but he sensed that they were if anything more bewildered by this mystery than he was himself. Although her appearance at Pine Lodge Motel was, on the face of it, suspicious he had been completely convinced that her stunned surprise at his blunt announcement about the finding of her husband's body had been the genuine article. There was something more than sexual passion and jealousy behind these killings. Clay was certain of it. At the moment he was like an archaeologist working on a digging who has unearthed a collection of broken fragments which seemed to have little relation to each other. He would go on probing, sifting, fitting together such pieces as he could and sooner or later the outline shape would become apparent. It was a question of time and patience. Clay had plenty of both.

He came forward into the room now, conscious of the atmosphere of tension and suspense. Evidently he had interrupted a very intense discussion. Mark was tightlipped, watchful and wary. Diana was deathly pale, hiding her hands in case he noticed their trembling. His quick eyes noted the glass on the drinks table, still with a residue of neat whisky at the bottom, a smear of lipstick at the brim. The ash-tray contained half a dozen cigarette butts, the same brand as he had observed in Mark Paxton's flat. The heavy curtains at the window had been drawn. The cushions of the sofa bore the indent of a form which had lain full length there not long ago.

'I'm sorry to disturb you, madam, but I particularly wanted to have a word with you about that phone call.'

Her eyelids blinked rapidly. For a moment she was speechless. He could hardly believe that it was relief he read on her face, yet he felt that she had been expecting and fearing a much more difficult question.

'Phone call? Oh – the one Geoffrey, my husband, was supposed to have made?'

'Yes, madam.'

Before he could define his question, Mark had stepped forward as if to draw Clay's fire on to himself.

'Have you discovered who made it?'

'No, we haven't, Mr Paxton. As a matter of fact—' Clay paused, still looking levelly at Diana. 'Mrs Stewart, correct me if I am mistaken, but I remember rightly you said that it was Mrs Bowen who received the call?'

'That's right,' Diana said, with a quick flick of her eyes towards Mark.

'That Mrs Bowen rushed round here and delivered the message to you?'

'Yes. That's quite right, Inspector.'

'Well, I'm sorry, madam, but that's not what Mrs Bowen says.'

The clock on the mantelpiece ticked a few seconds away, while Clay watched Diana with that slightly chiding but not unfriendly expression.

'Not what Mrs Bowen says?' Diana repeated uncomprehendingly.

'No,' Clay said, shaking his head. 'I'm afraid she doesn't confirm your story.'

'You mean there never was a phone call?' Mark demanded.

'Oh, yes. There was a phone call, sir.' Clay moved between them, advancing further into the room. He had heard a sound outside and wanted to be in a position where he would be facing anyone coming in through the door. By sheer coincidence he found himself by the table on which the telephone stood. 'But, according to Mrs Bowen, it was Mrs Stewart that received it.'

Diana's head snapped round towards Mark with a look of sudden surprise.

'She says', Clay pursued, 'that when she arrived here this morning you were in a state of great distress. You told her that you had just received a telephone call from your husband and didn't know what to do about it.'

'But that's not true!' Diana broke in. 'It simply isn't true.'

'Well, I'm sorry, but I'm only repeating what Mrs Bowen told me.'

Though Clay was himself reasonably convinced that Diana's instant denial had been the truth, he had a curious feeling that Mark was not so ready to believe her. The young man was studying her with a puzzled wrinkling of the brow. He turned now towards Clay.

'When did you see Mrs Bowen, Inspector?'

'This afternoon. Shortly after my visit to your flat, sir. It was just about the same time that shower of rain came on, if you're interested.'

Mark dropped his eyes at the faint rebuke, began to grope for another cigarette.

'I'd like to get to the bottom of this telephone call, Mrs Stewart.' Clay's voice had hardened, become more brisk and business-like. 'It seems to me to be important. If Mrs Bowen is not telling the truth she must have—'

Clay stopped. The handle of the door had been turned. A murmur of voices filtered in from the hall.

'Are you expecting anyone?' Mark asked Diana in a low voice.

'No. No one.'

Mrs Houston slipped through the partially opened door

with her customary expression of mingled triumph and disapproval.

'Excuse me, madam. It's Mr and Mrs Bowen.'

Clay happened to be watching Diana's profile at that moment. All his senses quickened to full stretch. It was one of those rare and precious instants when shock and surprise cause someone to lower all pretence. For some reason Mrs Houston's announcement had provoked in Diana a reaction which he could only describe in his own mind as superstitious terror.

He followed her gaze to the door. With Walter dancing attendance behind her, Thelma Bowen was standing on the threshold, as large as life and twice as fleshy.

CHAPTER IV

At the sight of Clay, Thelma had halted in her tracks. If Mrs Houston and Walter had not been filling the doorway behind her she might have made some excuse and departed again. As it was she recovered swiftly and as her eyes darted over the three occupants of the room, her face cracked into a forced smile.

'Hello, Inspector! We didn't realise you were here,' she said and advanced into the room.

She had changed, since Clay had last seen her, into a challengingly gay trouser suit which only served to emphasise even more Walter's wry remark about who wore the pants in that household. She had evidently done a careful job of work on her face, which was a little too heavily made up.

Clay started to say: 'I just popped in to have a word with Mrs Stewart—'

He broke off as he glanced towards Diana and in a couple of strides was beside her, holding her arm to steady her. Diana's face had gone ashen and she was swaying dangerously on her feet.

'What is it, Mrs Stewart?'

'I feel terribly odd,' Diana murmured. 'I think I'm going to—'

Suddenly her legs gave way. With a swift movement and a strength which surprised everyone Clay took her weight, gathering her up into his arms before she had time to fall. She lay with her head hanging limply and her legs dangling towards the floor.

Mark had dashed forward, but his help was hardly needed as Clay lowered Diana on to the settee. Thelma quickly arranged the cushions to support her head. Walter hovered helplessly in the background, then hurried over to the drinks table and began to pour out a glass of water. By the time he had brought it round to the front of the settee, Diana's eyelids were already beginning to flutter open again.

'Try and get her to drink this.'

Thelma frowned at Walter's presumption, but she took the glass and held it to Diana's lips. Diana put a hand up and sipped cautiously at the water. Almost as soon as they had opened her eyes had fixed on Thelma with a kind of horrified disbelief. Now she was shrinking further back into the cushions as if to escape from the concerned and solicitous face of her friend.

'Thelma! What's happened? What happened tonight?'

'What happened?' Thelma echoed, evidently quite nonplussed by Diana's question.

'Yes. How can you be here? I don't understand. I saw you at Kitty Tracy's. I thought you were—' She broke off and pushed the glass towards Mark. 'Please take this. I feel faint again—'

Knowing that Thelma was looking towards him for some enlightenment, Mark took the glass from Diana's hand and straightened up. He gripped Clay's arm and drew him away from the settee.

'I think we'd better get a doctor, don't you, Inspector?' he said, rather more loudly than was necessary. 'Which doctor does she have, Mrs Bowen?'

Thelma did not answer for the moment. She was staring across Diana's recumbent form at her husband. 'What? Oh, I think it's Dr Dickson – Alunbury 6270.'

'No, Mark, wait,' Diana said, struggling into a more upright position. 'There's no need for a doctor, really there isn't. I'll be all right.'

She turned towards Clay, endeavouring to produce a brave little smile. 'It was just a dizzy spell. I haven't been sleeping very well, I'm afraid.'

'No. I don't suppose you have, Mrs Stewart,' Clay agreed thoughtfully.

'I've been expecting this sort of thing to happen,' Walter announced with self-importance. 'I said to my wife only last night, if Diana doesn't crack up after all this, I said, it'll be nothing short of a miracle—'

Thelma's voice cut into his monologue like a whip-lash.

'Walter, go and tell Mrs Houston she's wanted.'

Walter stood with his mouth still open. Then he swallowed his resentment, turned to the door and went out into the hall.

'I think perhaps we ought to get her to bed,' Mark said. He was still nervous in case Diana should make some remark in front of Clay which would betray her visit to Kitty Tracy's shop.

'Yes. I think so too.' Thelma went to Diana and put her arm round her shoulders. 'Come along, my dear.'

Diana put her feet to the ground, then raised a hand to

her brow as her head began to spin again. 'I feel so terribly light-headed.'

'Let's get you upstairs. You'll feel better once you're in bed.'

With Mark on one side and Thelma on the other, Diana managed to struggle to her feet. Clay stood a little way apart, observing the scene but making no attempt to take any further part in it.

Mrs Houston materialised from the hall with Walter. Thelma gave her a meaningful look.

'Mrs Stewart doesn't feel very well, Mrs. Houston. We're putting her to bed.'

'Yes, of course!' Her lips pursed with disapproval, Mrs Houston went to Diana's side and firmly took possession of the arm which Mark had been holding. Her expression stated more clearly than any words that in a crisis of this kind she was the one who had the prior claim. 'Come along, Mrs Stewart.'

'Please don't fuss. It's nothing serious. I just fainted, that's all.'

'Yes, of course, dear,' Thelma agreed, humouring her friend.

On the way to the door Diana stopped to look round at Clay.

'I'm sorry about this, Inspector.'

'That's all right,' Clay assured her cheerfully. 'We'll continue our chat some other time.'

'Mr Paxton,' Diana tried to make her voice sound impersonal. 'I'll try and go through those papers with you tomorrow. Perhaps you could give me a ring.'

Mark replied with a stiff, unnatural little bow. 'Yes, of

course, Mrs. Stewart. Not to worry.'

The three men stood and watched while Diana, Mrs Houston and Thelma went out into the hall. Then Mark crossed the room to pick up his briefcase which he had left on the arm of one of the big chairs. Clay had moved to a commanding position in front of the fireplace.

Watching Mark, he said: 'Was Mrs Stewart feeling off colour earlier this evening, sir?'

'I honestly don't know,' Mark said, meeting the inspector's gaze with what he hoped was frank candour. 'I'd only been here about five minutes when you arrived. She phoned me about an hour ago and said she wanted to see me about some business.'

Clay's eyes registered the briefcase, which Mark was holding with self-conscious reverence. Then they swung to Walter.

'I take it yours was just a social call, Mr Bowen?'

'Well, no, not exactly.' Walter scratched the side of his bearded chin. 'My wife was very worried about what you told her, Inspector. About the telephone call, I mean. In the end we both thought it might be a very good idea if – well, if we had it out with Diana.'

'I don't think you'd have got very far, sir.'

'What do you mean?'

'Mrs Stewart still sticks to her story. She still maintains it was your wife who received that phone call.'

'But that isn't true!' Walter took an excited step forward. At that moment the telephone started to ring. 'I assure you it isn't! I was in all morning. If my wife had received the call I'd certainly have known about it.'

Clay made no comment. The phone bell rang another half-dozen times but none of the men made any move towards it. Then Clay cocked an eyebrow at Mark.

'I think you should answer, Mr Paxton. You can always take a message.'

A little reluctantly Mark hesitated and went to pick up the telephone.

'Alunbury 8130.'

'May I speak to Mrs Stewart, please?' The voice was that of a man. It was educated and authoritative and Mark felt that he had heard it before. But he could not put a name to it.

'I'm sorry, but it's a little difficult at the moment. Who is that, please?'

'That's not Paxton, is it?'

'Yes,' Mark said defensively, 'but I'm afraid I—'

'Thought I recognised your voice. My name's Mills. Nigel Mills, I'm Mrs Stewart's solicitor.'

'Oh, yes. I remember you now. We met in Geoffrey Stewart's office.'

'Is Mrs Stewart – ah – with you?'

'Mr Mills, I'm sorry, but Mrs Stewart has just had to go to bed. She's – she's not been feeling very well. Is there anything I can do?'

'No. I don't think so. I just wanted to—' Mills paused for a moment and Mark could hear an odd sucking noise which might have been the solicitor trying to revive a dying pipe. 'Well, I was going to ask Mrs Stewart if I could call round and see her some time tomorrow morning. It is rather urgent.'

'Perhaps I could give her a message.'

'Oh, no,' Mills said quickly. 'I – er. I'll leave it till I can see her myself. Maybe you could suggest a time?'

'Would, say ten thirty be all right? Here at Paddock Grange?'

'Yes. That would suit me admirably. You think she will be well enough?'

'Oh, I think so,' Mark said, wondering what made Mills sound so nervous and apologetic.

'Well, suppose we say ten thirty, unless you or she let me know to the contrary?'

'Yes. That should be all right.'

'Thank you, Mr Paxton. I'm – ah – much obliged to you.'

Mills sounded as if he had something more to add. Mark waited but all he heard was the receiver going down on its cradle.

Walter had edged a little closer, hoping to catch what the caller had been saying. Clay had not moved from his position by the fire, but he had produced a pipe and was thoughtfully thumbing tobacco into it from a leather pouch.

'That was Nigel Mills,' Mark explained. 'Something urgent he wants to see Mrs Stewart about. He's her solicitor, you know. I made an appointment for him to see her at ten thirty tomorrow morning.'

'Nigel Mills. I think I know him. Rather academic-looking chap of about fifty. About six foot, with steel-rimmed glasses and thinning grey hair. Always seems to be having trouble in getting his pipe to stay alight.'

'That's him,' Mark said with a laugh.

He saw Clay change his mind about his pipe and put it carefully away in his pocket. Thelma had opened the door and come back into the room.

'How is she?' Walter asked.

'I don't think it's anything serious, but she still complains of feeling dizzy. I left her because for some reason she seems nervous of people.'

'You didn't say anything about—?'

'No, I didn't, Walter,' Thelma said firmly. 'You can't talk to her about anything, not at the moment. She's not really with you.'

Turning a cold shoulder on Walter she faced Clay.

'You've probably guessed why we're here, Inspector?'

'I've just been talking to the inspector, Thelma,' Walter persisted, bobbing out from behind her. 'Diana still sticks to her story. She still thinks it was you who received that phone call.'

'She said that again – tonight?'

'Yes,' Clay confirmed. 'I'm afraid she did. Mrs Bowen, what did Mrs Stewart mean when she said, "I saw you at Kitty Tracy's"?'

Thelma glanced at Walter and shook her head in bewilderment. She did not seem embarrassed by the question but rather relieved that Clay had raised the matter.

'I don't know. I could not understand what she was talking about myself. She didn't make any further reference to it when we were upstairs.'

Clay nodded, apparently satisfied. Walter looked at Mark. 'Have *you* any idea what she meant, Mr Paxton?'

'None at all, I'm afraid.'

'Who is Miss Tracy, anyway?' Walter wanted to know.

'Well, Walter, the only Miss Tracy I know is the one in Station Road.'

'Oh, that little Irish woman who owns the sweet-shop!'

'That's right. I hardly know the woman, and I certainly haven't seen her for ages.'

Mark would have been glad of an opportunity to have a few more words with Diana but his hopes were frustrated when Clay asked for a lift back into Alunbury. He had sent the C.I.D. car back into town and walked up the Paddock Grange drive on foot.

Mark let Thelma move off first in her Hillman Imp before starting his estate car up and nosing down the tree-lined drive.

'Very practical machines, these,' Clay observed conversationally. 'You can carry a lot of stuff in the back.'

'Yes,' Mark agreed. He was uncomfortably aware that the large blanket with which he had covered Geoffrey's body was still on the floor of the rear compartment. 'I find it useful for golf clubs and trollies and that sort of thing. Actually the real reason I bought it was because I had rather a large dog.'

'Oh? What breed was it?'

'A red setter. She was a lovely animal.'

'You haven't got her any more?'

'No. She bit a delivery boy. I was taken to court and they ordered me to have her put down.'

Mark halted at the end of the drive, looked carefully in each direction before easing out into the main road. Clay had struck a match and was puffing smoke from his pipe.

'Does this bother you?'

'What?'

'My pipe smoke.'

'No. Not at all. I didn't know you smoked, though.'

'I smoke two or three pipes a day, that's all. Take good care not to smoke when there are women around. Learnt my lesson. I lit up in a restaurant one night and a girl told me off. Ye gods, she really tore me off a strip.' Clay chuckled at the recollection and lowered the window a few inches. 'Good-looking girl too.'

He threw his match out, wound the window up and glanced round at Mark.

'Mrs Stewart's a very good-looking woman, isn't she, sir?'

Mark kept his eyes fixed on the road ahead. 'Yes. I suppose she is. I hadn't really thought about it, Inspector.'

Clay settled back in his seat, puffing contentedly at his pipe. The two men exchanged no further conversation till they had passed the thirty-limit signs and the houses of Alunbury closed in on either side of them.

'You can drop me on the corner of Station Road, Mr Paxton. That'll do me nicely.'

Clay closed the door of Mark's car with considerate care and gave a friendly wave of the hand as the young man drove away. He stood on the corner of the pavement, watching the tail lights dwindle, noting the mud-spattered number-plate, the whiffle of a punctured exhaust pipe and the faint trail of blue smoke that the estate car left in its wake. Then he turned to walk down Station Road.

Clay was not hurrying. He wanted to think and he thought

best when he was walking, especially with an evenly burning pipe in his mouth. Station Road was one of the oldest streets in Alunbury and, since the new development in the town centre, one of the quietest. Traffic to the station was now carried by a broad boulevard a couple of hundred yards to the west. A good many of the shops here had gone out of business but there were still two or three antique shops which Clay prowled round when he had time to spare. He had to pass one on the way to Kitty Tracy's. Its windows were unlit but by the light of the street lamps he could see the glass-fronted mahogany corner-cupboard. It was so exactly like the one in his former home that he even wondered whether it could have found its way down here through trade channels.

Clay halted, staring into the shop window and for one of those rare moments the confident and efficient police officer was replaced by the lonely, regretful man. A flood of memories came flocking back to him. He stood, savouring them, till his pipe died on him. By that time he had decided that as soon as he had this case buttoned up he would come and buy that corner-cupboard.

A car passing along the street woke him from his brief reverie. He watched its reflection in the mirror. A Humber Sceptre driven by a hatless man with a cigarette drooping from his lip. Nothing significant about car or man but they were registered on Clay's memory and could be brought forward if ever needed. He extracted his pocket radio set, pulled out the aerial and called up the police station, leaving instructions for Sergeant Booth to locate Nigel Mills' address and telephone number and notifying him of Clay's present movements.

A good many aspects of the conversation in which he had taken part at Paddock Grange left him unsatisfied. Did those four honestly believe that an experienced police officer could be taken in by such evident deception? The interesting thing was that each couple had been as determined to fool the other two as they had been to pull the wool over the inspector's eyes. One particularly anomalous remark had awakened his curiosity and it was this that he had decided to follow up without delay.

The sign still hung on the inside of Kitty Tracy's door proclaiming to the outside world that her shop was CLOSED. The interior was in complete darkness. Not bothering to check whether he was observed or not, Clay took a handkerchief from his pocket and used it to turn the old-fashioned brass handle of the door. It opened inwards with a faint creak. He entered and closed the door behind him. He took a couple of steps into the shop and then stood there, letting his senses work for him. The light from the street filtered in, faintly illuminating the silent rows of glass containers on the shelves. A clinging smell of fried onions mingled with the sweet aroma of chocolates and lollipops. There was in the air the faintest tang of a woman's perfume. From somewhere in the gloom came the steady tick of a pendulum clock and a sound of small-scale asthmatic breathing.

Clay held his own breath and then expelled it slowly. He had spotted the big Persian cat enthroned on the top of one of the cabinets, its unblinking eyes fixed on him severely.

Now that his eyes had grown accustomed to the darkness

he moved to the counter, noted the bell used by customers to call for service, the convex glass bowl from which change could be scooped, the cash register still recording the last sale of seven pence.

He struck the bell. Its brassy chime was startlingly loud and vibrant. The resonant note died slowly in the silent shop. No one answered, but the cat rose, stretched itself and descended with a padded plop to the counter beside Clay's hand. It nuzzled the back of his hand, purring loudly and demanding to be caressed. He tickled it behind the ears, his eyes still roving round the shop. He waited half a minute and was about to strike the bell again when he spotted the dark wet stain on the back of his hand. Even in that light he could tell that it was blood and as the cat grinned up at him he saw that its jowl and whiskers were stained with the red moisture.

Perhaps sensing Clay's repugnance the cat suddenly jumped to the ground and with tail held high, galloped stiffly towards the stairway at the back of the shop. The hair on his scalp rising, Clay groped in his pocket for a torch and made to follow it.

Just as Diana had done, he almost knocked with his foot the knife lying on the floor. He directed the beam of his torch on to the object. It was a wicked-looking knife of the type that snaps open on a spring when the catch is released. The handle was of greyish bone, the blade slightly curved and tapering. The blood which stained it to the hilt was already partly dried.

Using his handkerchief once again to prevent his fingers from making contact with the knife handle, he picked it up and rapidly examined it. Then he replaced it carefully in the exact spot where he had found it and directed his torch up the staircase. Nobody lay sprawled on the stairs, no bloodstains marred the rather worn green stair-carpet.

Playing his torch ahead of him he went slowly up the stairs to the little landing. The door to the left, leading to the sitting room, was open. He stood on the threshold, probing the interior with his beam. It was obvious at once that the room had been ransacked with savage haste. The upholstery of the chairs had been slashed and the stuffing pulled out, the drawers of the desk had been smashed open and their contents upended on the floor, the fitted carpet had been pulled up round the edges of the room, even the back of the television set had been ripped off and the inside rifled.

Clay turned round and shone his torch on the doorway opposite the sitting room. The door had been kicked in, the lock splintering the woodwork away as it had yielded to brute force. From the interior a set of red prints left by the cat's feet led towards the stairs. Knowing already what he would find Clay crossed the landing and switched on the light by the door.

The bedroom had received the same treatment as the sitting room. The wardrobe had been stormed and its contents strewn on the floor, the contents of the drawers dumped on the floor, the curtains pulled away from the windows. The mattress and the bed itself had been slashed open, the stuffing yanked out. The floor was littered with beads, beads of every colour and size. Kitty Tracy herself lay hidden beneath a heap of blankets and clothing. The weals at her neck showed that she had put up a desperate struggle as her murderer tried to strangle her with her own necklaces. But the death wound had been the knife-thrust going in under her ribs. The blood had drained from her on to the imitation Chinese carpet and she was as pallid as a deep-frozen chicken.

Clay touched nothing, but for a minute let his eyes wander round the wrecked room. Then he took the radio from his breast pocket and slowly pulled out the aerial.

Nigel Mills' house was a solidly built late Victorian edifice in a residential road on the outskirts of Alunbury. The solicitor, who did very nicely out of his practice, lived in an old-world bachelor style. He opened the door himself in answer to Clay's knock and ring. He had changed for his solitary dinner and was wearing a plum-coloured velvet smoking-jacket. The steel-rimmed spectacles had been pushed up on to the top of his forehead and a struggling pipe was clenched between his teeth. Even with his slight stoop he topped Clay by several inches as he ushered him into a room which was part living room, part study, part library.

'It's very good of you to see me at such short notice, sir. I appreciate it.'

'That's all right, Inspector. Take a pew.'

Clay sat down in the leather armchair which Mills had indicated and stretched his legs towards a blazing log fire. The smell of Balkan Sobranie tobacco hung in the air. An open book had been laid, pages downward, on the arm of the solicitor's chair. Beside it, on a small table, stood a Waterford glass tumbler with a whisky and soda in it. Mills nodded at the glass.

'Can I offer you a drink?'

'I wouldn't say no to a Scotch and soda, sir.'

Mills went to a drinks cabinet built into the bookshelves which lined his room. He poured a generous measure of Bell's into a glass and splashed in soda.

Clay said: 'I believe you have an appointment with Mrs Stewart tomorrow morning, sir.'

Mills turned with the glass in his hand. He seemed faintly surprised and a little embarrassed at such a question. 'Yes, I have. And I can't say I'm looking forward to it.'

'No, sir?'

'Definitely not, Inspector. But how did you know about the appointment?'

'I was at the house when you telephoned.'

'Oh. Oh, I see.'

Still puzzled, Mills brought the drink to Clay. The inspector nodded his thanks and waited till the other man had picked up his own drink before taking a sip. It was a good and strong one and he felt it run warmly down inside him. He sank back further into the chair and relaxed. This was just what he needed after that macabre discovery in Kitty Tracy's shop. When he'd left the place it had been crawling with policemen, both in uniform and plain clothes. A reluctant Sergeant Booth had been left in charge, with instructions to go through the chaos with a fine tooth comb.

'What can I do for you, Inspector?' Mills enquired after what he considered a decent pause. Instead of sitting down he preferred to stand with his back to the fire, warming his legs.

Clay nodded towards the evening paper which had been cast to the floor beside Mills' chair. 'I imagine you've read about this afternoon, sir? About Mrs Stewart – the motel?'

'Yes. An appalling business. Have you any idea who did it?'

'Yes, sir. Since you ask me – I have.'

Mills' eyebrows expressed his surprise at this frank answer. He decided to sit down in his chair after all. Having done that he looked at Clay, evidently expecting him to elaborate.

But Clay went on: 'Now may I ask you a question, Mr Mills?'

'Certainly. Go ahead.'

'I understand your firm acted for Mr Stewart.'

'Yes, we did a certain amount of work for him. But I'm afraid he was rather an unsatisfactory client.' Mills put his glass down and started to feel in his pocket for matches. 'What is it you're curious about, Inspector? What is it you want to know?'

'I'm curious about his will, sir.'

'His will?'

'I'd like to know who the beneficiaries are.'

Mills hesitated, a match held between his fingers. 'Then I suggest you ask Mrs Stewart tomorrow. She'll be able to tell you.'

'I'm asking you, sir,' Clay said pleasantly. 'And I don't want to know tomorrow morning. I want to know now – tonight.'

Obviously playing for time in which to decide what was the proper thing for him to do, Mills struck his match and used it to coax his Dunhill pipe into some semblance of life. Clay heard the same optimistic sucking noise as had filtered down the telephone wires to Mark Paxton's ears.

'Mr Mills.' Clay put his glass down and leant forward in his chair. 'A moment ago you asked me if I knew who the murderer was and I was frank with you. I said I did.'

'Well?'

'Well – don't you think, in the circumstances, you might stretch a point too, sir, and take me into your confidence?'

Mills inspected the interior of his pipe bowl, contemplated Clay thoughtfully, then placed the Dunhill carefully in a heavy wooden ash-tray. Then he got up, crossed the room to his desk and opened one of the drawers. He took out a foolscap-sized envelope. When he came back to the rug in front of the fireplace, Clay had risen to face him.

'Just over two years ago,' Mills said, 'Mr and Mrs Stewart came to see me. They'd been married about eighteen months and Geoffrey, Mr Stewart, said he wanted to make a new will. We discussed the details and eventually I drew up the document. With the exception of one bequest – a thousand pounds to his housekeeper – he left everything to his wife.'

Mills was gazing at the inspector with a worried expression, his high brow wrinkled.

'Go on, sir.'

'Well, about a month ago I had a call from Geoffrey Stewart saying that he wanted to see me on a matter of urgent business. I went round to his office and he presented me with this envelope. He said it contained a new will – one he'd just had drawn up – and he didn't want his wife or anyone else to know about it.'

'Yes, sir?' Clay prompted again, as Mills paused.

'I took the envelope away with me and placed it in a private deed box. This evening when I heard that his body had been found I took it out and brought it home with me.'

The seal had been broken and the flap opened so Clay could assume that Mills had already perused the contents.

'Was he telling the truth?'

'Yes. He was telling the truth all right.' Mills pulled the steel-rimmed glasses from the top of his forehead on to the bridge of his nose and slid the folded sheet of thick parchment from the envelope. 'The will was drawn up by a firm of solicitors in London – a thoroughly reputable firm, I might add. It was signed in their office on July 10th, just five weeks ago.'

Mills was studying the second page of the document. He did not offer to hand it to Clay.

'Well?'

'He's left a thousand pounds to the housekeeper,' Mills said slowly, 'nine thousand pounds to his wife, and the residue of his estate to Miss Diana Valesco, of 33, Franklin Terrace, Chelsea, London, S.W.I.'

Mills had been reading the name and address from the will itself. He slipped his glasses on to the top of his forehead again. He seemed shocked by the enormity of what he had just read out. He replaced the will in its envelope and put it down on the table.

'The residue of his estate,' Clay repeated the phrase. 'Have you any idea of what that would amount to, sir?'

'Somewhere in the region of a quarter of a million pounds.'

A log fell out of the fire. Mills stooped to pick up the tongs and put it back in the grate.

'Diana. You did say Diana?'

'I did. Miss Diana Valesco. It's a strange coincidence, is it not?'

'Diana Valesco.' Clay spoke the name almost angrily. 'Who the devil is she?'

Mills straightened up and gave the inspector a wry look.

'That's precisely what Mrs Stewart's going to ask me tomorrow. I wish I knew the answer.'

Franklin Terrace was a row of solidly constructed Edwardian houses. Like most of them, number 33 had been converted to form three self-contained flats. Miss Diana Valesco, as a neat card beside the bell-push confirmed, inhabited the one on the first floor.

Clay was unfamiliar with London, but he had read plenty of reports about the place and about Chelsea in particular. It did not surprise him that at an hour of the night when Alunbury was cosily bedded down the denizens of Chelsea were evidently just starting on the night's revels. The drive up from Alunbury and the search for a parking space had taken him something over an hour. To his surprise, number 33, Franklin Terrace was crisply clean and well-lit. He had half expected to find furtive-looking men sheepishly emerging from sleazy flatlets. Instead, through an uncurtained window in the ground-floor flat, he could see a silvery-haired woman playing a grand piano.

The heavy black front door was locked. Clay pressed the bell beside the card which bore Diana Valesco's name. He had to wait a full minute before a voice spoke in the loudspeaker set in the wall.

'Yes. Who is it, please?'

Even in that brief phrase the owner of the voice betrayed her foreign origin.

'Miss Valesco?'

'Yes.'

'My name is Clay. Detective-Inspector Clay.'

'You are – from the police?'

'That's right. May I see you for a few moments please?'

'Yes. Yes, of course.' Miss Valesco sounded a little put out. 'Please come up. I will open the door.'

There came a click and a buzz. The heavy door sprang open a few inches. Clay pushed through. He mounted newly carpeted stairs to the first-floor landing. As he reached it the door of the flat opened.

Clay was halted in his tracks. Diana Valesco had the sumptuous beauty of one of Botticelli's Florentine models. She was wearing a silk housecoat hastily knotted round her waist. Her dark hair fell in glistening waves down her back. She was clutching a handkerchief in her hand. Clay surmised from the redness surrounding her eyes that she had been crying.

Noticing her nervousness he produced a card from his wallet and offered it to her. She studied it uncertainly and handed it back to him. Clay put the card and the wallet carefully away and took off his hat. Reluctantly she moved back into the hallway, holding the door for him with downcast eyes.

'Please come in.'

The loudspeaker had distorted the soft, musical quality of her voice.

'Thank you. I'm sorry to disturb you at such a late hour, Miss Valesco.'

Slightly off balance for once, Clay walked into the large sitting room which looked out over Franklin Terrace. It was evident at once that this was the room of a person with excellent taste and a flair for colour. The furniture was in the less obtrusive modern style, but bright and gay. An obviously sophisticated set of hi-fi equipment had been built into the far corner of the room. On the centre table a large colour photograph of Geoffrey Stewart was displayed unashamedly. It was a happy, laughing photograph of a completely relaxed Geoffrey in holiday clothes.

'What a delightful room!' Clay remarked in surprise.

'Thank you.' Diana Valesco smiled faintly, studying the inspector and trying to work out why he had been expecting to find something so very different.

Clay went straight to the photograph and picked it up. He could see now that some words had been scribbled in biro across the bottom corner. 'With all my love, Geoffrey.'

'That is why you have come?' she asked from behind him. 'Because of – Geoffrey?'

He put the photograph frame down gently and turned to face her.

'Yes. I take it you've heard the news?'

She nodded, her fist closing tightly on the handkerchief. 'I heard this evening. It was on the radio. Then I went out and bought an evening newspaper.'

Her mouth was trembling. Her eyes, when they flickered up to his face, were moist.

'Miss Valesco,' Clay said quickly in his business tone, 'I'm investigating this case and I think – in fact, I feel sure that you can help me.'

'I'll tell you anything you want to know.'

'Thank you. Now, can you tell me—'

'But first, please,' she cut in, 'you must answer for me a question. How did you find out about me? How did you know to come to this address?'

'It was in the will,' Clay said quietly.

'The will?' Her pronunciation of the word made it sound like 'wheel'. One eyebrow had lifted and she was meeting his eyes directly. The impact of her own was disquieting in its femininity. Clay, who had recently been confronted by the rather brittle and insincere good looks of Geoffrey's wife, could understand the fascination which this Italian girl might have had for him.

'Mr Stewart's will. He made a new one quite recently.'

'And my name – it is mentioned in this will?'

'Yes. It is. You seem surprised.'

'But I am, very surprised.'

No eyes could have expressed a more innocent astonishment. Clay, who sometimes found it hard to judge the character of women, was already convinced that the obviously well-educated Miss Valesco was no opportunist.

'Yes, well—' He turned to walk away towards the window, struggling to keep this interview on an unemotional basis. 'That's not why I came here. You'll hear about the will later from someone else. Tell me about your friendship with

Mr Stewart. When did you first meet him? How did you meet?'

'We met about six months ago.'

'Where?'

'Here – in London.'

'In Chelsea?'

Diana Valesco nodded, the beginnings of a sadly reminiscent smile tugging at the corners of her mouth.

'Yes. In the middle of the King's Road.'

It was close to midnight when Clay descended the stairs of 33, Franklin Terrace and let himself out through the heavy door. By that time he had been continually on this job for sixteen hours with intervals of no more than a few minutes for quick snatches of food. He realised that he had no chance of being back at Kitty Tracy's place by midnight, which was the time he had given Sergeant Booth.

He found a telephone kiosk two blocks away from Franklin Terrace. He dialled the code for Alunbury and the number of Kitty Tracy's shop. Presently Booth's voice answered cautiously.

'Yes. Who is it?'

'Sar'nt Booth. Clay here.'

'Oh, hello, sir. We wondered what had happened to you. Where are you speaking from?'

'I'm in London. A new lead's opened up and I had to come and interview someone. What about your end? Have you found anything?'

'Yes, sir,' Booth said wearily. 'We've found plenty. Before

we could start a proper search we had to tidy this mess up. That took us a good hour. Ye gods, whoever did this must have—'

'Anything of special interest?' Clay cut in impatiently.

'Well, as a matter of fact, yes. Several interesting things. But whether what we've found is the same thing as the murderer was looking for, I wouldn't like to say.'

'So what have you found?' Clay's fingers were drumming with impatience on the glass window of the kiosk.

'I'm not sure that I ought to—' Booth hesitated, then added mysteriously: 'Could we discuss this later, sir?'

'Yes, all right, Booth.' Stifling his curiosity Clay accepted the sergeant's decision not to talk about this openly over the telephone. 'I make it just on midnight. It'll take me a good hour to get back to Alunbury. I think we'd better meet in my office, Booth.'

'Very good, sir,' Booth said with weary resignation. 'I'll be waiting for you any time after one.'

It was three a.m. before Clay got to bed on that Wednesday night. He was back at the police station by eight, and nine o'clock found him turning into the forecourt of Tallboys' garage in one of the C.I.D. enquiry cars. He parked it neatly in a place where it would not impede the entry and exit of cars pulling in to refuel at the pumps.

Vince was just hanging up the nozzle after filling up a customer's car.

'Is Mr Tallboys in?' Clay called over to him.

The attendant jerked his head towards a door at the far

end of the showroom. 'I think he's in his workshop.'

Clay started to walk past the big plate-glass windows behind which was displayed Ned Tallboys' selection of exotic second-hand cars. It was one of those whitely bright English mornings, when the sunlight is reflected by huge billowing white clouds sailing majestically across the blue sky. A morning for dreaming of the open road, European motorways and continental touring. Despite himself, Clay paused, staring through the window with the covetous concentration of a boy contemplating the purchase of his first bicycle. He wondered, if he suddenly found himself winner of the Premium Bond jackpot, which of these cars he would choose. Passing over the white Triumph Stag, the red Alfa Romeo 1750 and a very slinky Lotus Europa, he was considering a very beautiful Maserati when he suddenly realised that Ned Tallboys' sales manager was grinning at him from a desk at the back of the showroom.

Banishing his pipe-dream, Clay turned briskly towards the door of Tallboys' private workshop.

The garage owner glanced up when the inspector pushed the door open and flashed him a quick welcoming smile. He had put on a white coat over his countrified tweed suit and with a screwdriver in his hand was tinkering with a car radio set. The work-bench was littered with various articles on which he had been amusing himself – a walkie-talkie radio, a carburettor, a tape-recorder and numerous cannibalised engine parts. An open packet of cigarettes and a lighter lay on the edge of the work-bench.

'Good morning, Mr Tallboys,' Clay said in his most friendly tone. 'Can you spare me a minute?'

Ned put his screwdriver down and straightened up, automatically flicking an imaginary speck from the lapel of his overall coat.

'Yes, of course. Come along in, Inspector. What can I do for you?'

Clay searched for an uncluttered and clean place on which to place his hat and then decided it would be more hygienic to hold on to it. 'I'm making enquiries about a woman called Miss Tracy. She has a sweet-shop, or rather I should say—'

'Kitty Tracy?' Ned cut in.

'Yes, sir.'

'I know Kitty Tracy. She's a tenant of mine.'

Clay nodded without surprise. 'So I understand, sir.'

'Has something happened to her, Inspector?'

There was an upended packing case against the wall of the workshop. A quick inspection showed Clay that it was free of oil and grease spots.

'May I sit down?'

'Yes, of course.'

Clay lowered his weight carefully on to the packing case, which withstood the burden. Ned watched him, tapping the screwdriver against the palm of his hand.

'Miss Tracy was murdered last night. She was stabbed to death. According to the doctor's report—'

'Kitty Tracy?' Ned interrupted incredulously. 'No. No. I don't believe it.'

'I'm afraid it's true, sir.'

'But why on earth should anyone want to murder her?'

'I can't imagine why. That's the reason for my being here,

sir. I'm hoping you might be able to help me answer that question.'

Ned moved a few paces to replace the screwdriver in its slot on one of his tool shelves. 'I'll certainly help you if I can, Inspector. What is it you want to know?'

'How well were you acquainted with Miss Tracy?'

'Oh, I hardly knew her at all, Inspector. About two years ago I bought some property in Station Road; Kitty Tracy's shop and Felton's the newsagents. It was purely an investment on my part. I didn't want possession of the property.'

Clay nodded his comprehension of the subtle distinction.

'At first Miss Tracy was a very difficult tenant. She seemed convinced that it was my intention to evict her, which was quite untrue. I can't imagine what she thought I was going to do with a grubby little sweet-shop.'

Ned laughed shortly and reached towards the cigarette package.

'What do you mean when you say she was difficult, sir?'

'She refused to pay her rent unless certain repairs were carried out and she wrote me a couple of absolutely stinking letters about it.'

'Have you got the letters?'

'No. I'm afraid I haven't. I threw them away. I don't want to sound unkind, Inspector, but she was a bit dotty, you know. No one took her seriously.'

'Someone did, sir,' Clay pointed out. 'Otherwise why was she murdered?'

Tallboys stuck the cigarette in his mouth and clicked the lighter into flame.

'Yes. I see what you mean.'

He stood looking thoughtfully down at the inspector, drawing deep on the cigarette. Suddenly conscious of his rudeness he picked up the packet and offered it to his guest. Clay shook his head, but took out his own pipe and pouch.

'Mr Tallboys, if I take you into my confidence, will you be perfectly frank with me about something?'

'Why, er, yes,' Ned said, assuming his most frank expression.

'I think Kitty Tracy was blackmailing Mr Stewart,' Clay said, thumbing tobacco carefully into his pipe. 'I think she'd been blackmailing him for some time.'

'Kitty Tracy blackmailing Geoffrey Stewart?'

'Yes.'

'But that's absurd.'

Ned placed his cigarette on the top of a vice and twisted a tall stool out from under the bench. He sat down on it, his long face serious and bewildered.

'I don't think so,' Clay went on. 'It's my bet that during the past twelve months she's had close on two thousand pounds from him.'

'What was she blackmailing him about?'

Clay drew the flame from his match into the pipe-bowl half a dozen times and squinted up at Ned. 'Don't you know, Mr Tallboys?'

'No,' Ned said with an emphatic shake of his head. 'I do not.'

Clay's pipe was going well now. He laid the match down meticulously on the edge of the work-bench, his eye resting for a moment on the broken tape-recorder. Then he settled himself more comfortably on the packing case as if he intended to be there for some time.

'Several days ago – the day Mr Stewart was murdered in fact – I asked you how long you'd known him. You said ten years.'

'Well?'

'Ten years is a long time. You can get to know a man very well in ten years.'

'What are you suggesting, old man?' Ned enquired easily, recovering his cigarette from the vice.

'Did you know he was having an affair with a girl named Diana Valesco?'

Tallboys hesitated before answering. The two men were facing each other, the smoke from Clay's pipe billowing out challengingly to meet the cigarette smoke. 'Well, I knew there was a doll somewhere in the background, but he never told me who she was.'

'He just told you he had a girl-friend?'

'No. He didn't even tell me that. He—' Ned threw his cigarette on to the ground and twisted his foot over it. 'Well, to be perfectly honest I saw him one night. It was up in Town, at a night club. He was with a dark, good-looking girl. They were dancing cheek to cheek and – Well, it wasn't very hard to get the message.'

'Why didn't you tell me about this before, Mr Tallboys?'

'I – I just didn't think it was important.'

Clay had taken the pipe out of his mouth. His eyes were

snapping and the friendly tone had gone from his voice.

'You must have known this information was important, sir.'

Ned shrugged his shoulders contritely. He had begun to look very ashamed of himself. 'Yes, well, I'm sorry, Inspector.'

'You did not want to get involved,' Clay suggested icily. 'Is that it?'

Ned bit back whatever he was going to say and nodded his agreement.

'Did you tell Stewart you had seen him?' Clay pursued.

'Well, I hinted at it.'

'What does that mean?'

Uncomfortable now, Ned shifted his weight on the stool. 'We had a few words one day about a car I'd lent him. He was the sort of driver who shows no consideration for an engine and – I told him he ought to stick to dancing.'

'And what did he say to that?'

'Oh, he just laughed it off. But he knew what I meant, all right.' Ned stood up and began to take off the white coat he had worn to protect his clothes. 'What did you say this girl was called, the girl I saw him with?'

'Well, if it's the same girl her name's Valesco. Diana Valesco. She's an Italian.'

'That's her all right. Smashing figure, dark, very good-looking.'

'Yes,' Clay agreed, his memory clicking back without effort to the girl in 33, Franklin Terrace.

'Quite a dish, in fact.' Ned shook his head in rueful wisdom. 'But, by George, I'll bet she was expensive!'

Clay drew evenly on his pipe, listening to Tallboys' enthusiastic descriptions tolerantly.

'I don't think you've got the right picture, sir.'

'No?'

'No. Mr Stewart was serious about this girl. Very serious. He's even mentioned her in his will.'

'You mean, he's left her something?'

Clay stood up and put his hat on his head. It was clear that as far as he was concerned the interview was finished. He smiled at Ned's deeply concerned face.

'Only the jackpot, sir.'

In the drawing room at Paddock Grange Mark and Diana were facing each other. Her eyes were red-rimmed and there were black shadows under them. For once she did not seem to have taken the trouble over her appearance. Her skin was a little blotchy, her nose shiny and rather pink. Mark's fists were clenched, his eyes distant and hostile.

'Now, come on, Diana. I want you to tell me exactly what he said.'

'But I've told you,' Diana protested. She began to turn away from him but he took a quick pace forward, seizing her roughly by the arm and forcing her round.

'You keep telling me what you think. I don't want to know what you think. I want to know precisely—'

'Mark, you're hurting my arm.'

'I want to know precisely what Mills said.'

'Mark, please—'

Diana's face was twisting with pain. It was evident that she was on the verge of tears again. A moment passed and then he released her arm. She began to rub the place with her other hand.

'Geoffrey made a new will,' she stated tonelessly.

'When?'

'About a month ago.'

'Did Mills draw it up?'

'No. It was done in London by a firm called – Belton and Rice, I think he said.'

Mark nodded. 'I know Belton and Rice. Our firm has had dealings with them. They're very reputable.'

'That's what Nigel Mills said.'

'Well – go on,' Mark commanded.

'That's all there is to it. He left Mrs Houston a thousand pounds. He left me nine thousand. All the rest goes to this girl.'

'Everything?'

'Yes, everything. I mean that, Mark. Literally everything. Nigel said he reckoned it must be two hundred and fifty thousand.'

'I don't believe it,' Mark said softly. He subsided on to the arm of the sofa. His face had gone a shade paler. 'I just don't believe it.'

'It's true, Mark.'

He rounded on her accusingly. 'Did you know about this girl?'

'No. Of course I didn't!'

'You'd never even heard of her?'

'No. I hadn't heard of her,' Diana reiterated angrily. 'If I'd heard of her don't you think I'd have told you about her?'

He stood up again, paced restlessly to the window embrasure and stood looking out.

'My God, after all what's happened! After all we've been through this week!'

'Mark, what are we going to do?'

He did not answer at once. She stared at his back, fighting down the sense of solitude and panic which threatened to engulf her. Suddenly he swung round.

'There's only one thing you can do. Contest the will.'

'But surely that could take months.'

'It doesn't matter how long it takes. You've got to do it.' He strode towards her. 'Now, listen Diana, first thing tomorrow morning I—'

Abruptly he stopped. He was looking at her but his eyes were not really seeing her. A peculiar detached expression had come over his face, an expression she had seen once before.

'What is it?'

He did not answer. With deliberate slowness he took out a cigarette and lit it. He seemed to have forgotten her very existence.

'Mark, what is it?' she asked again, trying to prevent the fear from coming into her voice.

He came out of his trance enough to register her presence.

'What did Mills say she was called, this girl?'

'Valesco. By some strange chance her Christian name is the same as mine.'

'Diana Valesco. Did he say where she lives?'

'Somewhere in Chelsea. Franklin Terrace, I think he said.'

His thoughts were once more moving away from her.

When he looked at her again it was with that disquieting expression which gave her the unnerving impression that she was little more than a wax dummy.

'Mark, what is it?' she said for the third time.

At once his manner changed and softened. The old affection was back on his face and when he took her arm it was with gentle fingers.

'Diana, I want you to forget what I said just now. I don't want you to do anything. I don't want you to do anything for forty-eight hours. You understand?'

She looked up into his eyes. In this mood, with all the charm and persuasiveness switched on, he had the power to twist her round his little finger. 'Yes. All right, Mark.'

He bent to kiss her lightly, gave her arm a reassuring squeeze and turned on his heel. From the doorway he did not look back, so he did not see the expression on her face. Fright and bewilderment had given way to a look of speculation and resolve.

Diana Valesco was packing. She had spent the early part of the afternoon at the travel agency and had managed to procure a seat on an Alitalia night flight to Milan. Now, with a record of Respighi's *Fountains of Rome* on her gramophone, she was selecting the clothes she would need for a fortnight in the Dolomites.

She was going through from her bedroom to the sitting room to collect Geoffrey's photograph when the telephone started to ring. She paused, eyeing it doubtfully. There was no one in England now to whom she had any desire to speak.

Her one desire and instinct was to escape from this hateful country and take refuge amongst the mountains where she had spent her childhood. But Inspector Clay had said that he might telephone her and she had promised him her help. There had been something comforting and reassuring about him. She had been forced to revise completely her ideas of police officers.

She turned the hi-fi down and went to pick up the scarlet telephone receiver.

'Chelsea 2975.'

She waited, hearing the familiar sounds of someone grappling with the intricacies of a public call-box. Then a voice which she did not remember hearing before.

'Could I speak to Miss Valesco, please?'

'Who is that, please?'

'My name is Paxton. Mark Paxton. I'm a friend, or rather I was a friend of Geoffrey Stewart's.'

The tone of the voice was carefully modulated and she was familiar enough with England to be able to tell that he was well educated. But some womanly instinct was alerted by his over-confident manner.

She paused a moment before saying: 'This is Diana Valesco speaking.'

'Oh. Good afternoon, Miss Valesco,' the voice continued smoothly. 'I'm terribly sorry to trouble you, but – do you think we could possibly meet some time? There's something I'd very much like to talk to you about.'

'Well, it is a little difficult,' she hedged. 'I am going away from London this evening – or rather later tonight. Is it urgent, Mr – I'm afraid I did not quite catch your name.'

'Paxton. Yes, I'm afraid it really is rather urgent. Believe me, Miss Valesco, I wouldn't dream of troubling you if it wasn't important. What time are you departing?'

'About nine or ten o'clock.'

'Could we meet somewhere for a drink? It would be a pleasure to—'

'No,' she said quickly. 'That is impossible. Could you come— Could you come here before dinner. I'm afraid I won't have very long to—'

'That would be fine. What about seven o'clock? Is that convenient for you?'

'Yes. Seven o'clock,' she agreed, feeling that once again she had too easily allowed herself to be talked into doing something against her better judgment. 'My address is—'

'I've got the address,' Mark reassured her. 'Thirty-three, Franklin Terrace, Chelsea.'

'Yes, that's right.'

'Thank you, Miss Valesco.'

She put the telephone down thoughtfully, went to pick up the photograph and stared at it with intensity. If he had not said he was a friend of Geoffrey's she would never have consented to see him. She glanced at her watch. Five-fifteen. She would have to hurry to get her packing done and the flat tidied up before her guest arrived.

Mark was a good ten minutes late in keeping his appointment with Diana Valesco. He had run up the stairs and was breathing heavily as he waited for her to answer his ring. She took quite a long time coming and he was about to press the bell-push a second time when he heard her footsteps and the door was opened.

'Miss Valesco?'

'Yes.'

'I'm Mark Paxton.'

He was smiling with pleasure at the sight of such a very attractive girl. She was wearing calf-hugging white boots, a suede skirt and an aquamarine blue man-styled shirt with patch pockets. The slightly severe quality of her clothes simply served to emphasise her womanliness. She seemed a little distraught and he wondered whether she might have even forgotten that he was coming.

'Oh, yes. Yes, of course. I'm sorry. Please come in, Mr Passtown.'

'Thank you,' Mark said, giving her an appreciative glance.

His eyes registered the movement of her hips as she preceded him into the sitting room.

'Would you excuse me for a moment?' She had stopped in the centre of the room and was biting the inside of her lip nervously. 'I won't be a moment.'

'Yes, of course,' Mark said easily.

She escaped through a door which he rightly assumed led to her bedroom and he began to wonder what might be coming next. Old Geoffrey had certainly known how to pick them.

He began to make a more careful inspection of the room, noting the hi-fi equipment, the row of Italian and English paperbacks, the fashion magazines on the table, the broad divan with a score of blazingly colourful scatter cushions. From the telephone set beside the window came a faint tinkle as if the receiver had been replaced on an extension in some other room.

Mark felt for his case and thoughtfully put a cigarette between his lips. Before he could light it, he heard the bedroom door re-open. He turned expectantly and the lighter slipped from his hand to the floor.

Clay smiled at the expression of bewilderment on the young man's face.

'Good evening, Mr Paxton.'

Mark pulled himself together and to cover his embarrassment stooped to recover the lighter. When he straightened up his face was flushed.

'I didn't expect to find you here, Inspector.'

'No, I don't expect you did, sir,' Clay agreed comfortably. 'Won't you sit down?'

With a confidence which seemed to indicate that he had been here long enough to feel at home, Clay waved a hand to the settee.

'I had an appointment with Miss Valesco and when she told me you were dropping in on her I— Well, I wanted to have a chat with you so I thought we might as well have it here as anywhere else.'

Mark sat gingerly on the edge of the wide settee. Its springs gave beneath his weight and he found himself sitting in an awkwardly hunched position.

'What is it you wanted to have a chat about?'

Clay turned a chair round to face the settee before he answered.

'Mrs Stewart.'

'Mrs Stewart?' Mark echoed, counterfeiting surprise.

'Yes, sir. How long have you known Mrs Stewart, Mr Paxton?'

The question had been put in an easy, conversational tone. Mark replied in the same vein.

'About two or three years, I suppose.'

'Would you say she was a close friend of yours?'

'Good heavens, no!' Mark exclaimed, laughing. 'Naturally I've seen quite a lot of her recently, but she's certainly not a close friend, Inspector.'

Clay took an envelope from his pocket. He did not hand it to Mark but the latter could see it well enough to recognise the note scribbled across it as his own handwriting.

'Then would you mind explaining something to me?'

'Certainly, if I can.'

'If she's not a friend of yours,' Clay was looking down at the message on the envelope with a frown, 'why did you take her to the theatre – the Criterion Theatre – on the night of March 18th?'

'March 18th?'

'That's right, sir.

'I didn't.'

'I think you did, sir. You took Mrs Stewart to the theatre and you had dinner together at a little restaurant in Soho called the Lago Endine – just the two of you.'

'That's right!' Mark exclaimed, after a short pause. He was smiling, as if grateful to the inspector for reminding him. 'You're absolutely right, Inspector. That was the night Mr

Stewart was taken ill. Well, not really ill. He had a bilious attack. He was taking his wife to the theatre and at the last moment had to cry off and—'

Mark seemed to have run out of enthusiasm. Clay was listening with that courteous, attentive and slightly surprised expression which made him so difficult to lie to. His eyes had a disconcerting way of moving from the face to some other part of the body which was betraying tension. They had switched now to Mark's hands, which were twiddling the still unlighted cigarette.

'Go on, sir.'

'So he telephoned me and asked me if I'd take her instead,' Mark finished lamely.

'Wasn't that a little unusual?' Clay made the suggestion with diffidence.

'Yes. It was. I was very surprised. Actually I had a date with someone else. But there was nothing I could do about it. The boss's wife? I hadn't much choice, had I, Inspector?'

Mark laughed disarmingly. The inspector put the envelope back into his pocket. The corners of his mouth twitched with what might have been a sympathetic smile. He appeared quite satisfied with Mark's explanation.

'Yes. I get the point. Thank you, Mr Paxton, that explains it.'

Relieved that the awkward moment had passed, Mark lit his cigarette and disposed himself more comfortably on the settee.

'How did you find out about the theatre?'

'I'm investigating a murder case, sir.' Just for once Clay's tone and expression were deadly serious. 'I have to find out all sorts of things, ask all kinds of questions. And when people try to hide the truth from me I naturally begin to wonder why.'

'I see. Well, just to keep the record straight, I'm not having a wild affair with Mrs Stewart.' Looking straight into Clay's eyes, Mark put on his frankest smile. 'If that's what you're thinking, Inspector.'

Wooden-faced, Clay let the suggestion hang in the air. After a short pause he said: 'Tell me about Miss Valesco, sir.'

'What do you mean?'

'How did you hear about her?'

'Mr Stewart made a will and apparently he left most of his money to—'

'Yes. I know about the will, sir.'

'Well, that's how I heard about Miss Valesco. Nigel Mills, the solicitor, saw Mrs Stewart and she sent for me.'

'Why?'

'She – she wants me to have a talk with Miss Valesco. She wants me to try and come to some arrangement with her.'

'About the will?'

'Yes.'

'But isn't that a job for a lawyer? I should have thought that Mr Mills was the person to discuss—'

'I'm afraid Mrs Stewart is not particularly fond of lawyers at the moment, Inspector,' Mark said tartly. He got up abruptly and went past Clay's shoulder to tap his cigarette ash into a Venetian glass ash-tray on the centre table.

Clay gave a little nod towards the place where Mark had been sitting. 'I see what you mean.'

'Now, may I ask you a question?'

'Of course.'

'Why did you come here this evening?'

'I should have thought that was obvious. I came to see Miss Valesco.'

'But why?'

Clay rose unhurriedly from his chair and walked slowly towards the door by which Mark had entered. The latter watched him uncomprehendingly, until he saw that the inspector's hat, coat and gloves had been laid on a chair just behind the door. Clay threw his coat over one arm, tossed his gloves into his hat and, holding it in his hand, turned back to direct the full brunt of a humourless stare at Mark.

'Geoffrey Stewart was shot, Ken Harding was beaten to death, Kitty Tracy was stabbed. All three were murdered.'

'Yes, we know about that,' Mark said guardedly, his eyes hooding as he waited for whatever was coming next. Experience had taught him that Clay's exit lines usually had a sting in them.

'And I'd like to make quite sure, sir, that the same thing isn't going to happen to Miss Valesco.'

CHAPTER V

The C.I.D. department of Alunbury police station was in full operation all round the clock. With three separate murders to investigate, their resources were stretched to the limit. Clay had taken his team of detective sergeants and detective constables off all less important enquiries to concentrate them on the sudden eruption of criminal violence which had shattered the cosy peacefulness of Alunbury. To say that the atmosphere of the market town was one of panic would have been an exaggeration, but householders were making sure that their doors and windows were fastened before retiring for the night, those who walked the lonely streets after dark had taken to casting nervous glances over their shoulders and the local paper had started a campaign of criticism against the inefficiency of the police. Their headline on this Friday morning, in sixty-four point type, was WHO NEXT?

In the office of Mr Jarman across the corridor from Clay's office, Booth was sitting alone amongst the filing cabinets. He had the telephone to one ear and was stopping the other with his massive index finger. His expression was tense.

'Yes. I'm ready. Go ahead.'

The line was live. He could hear the faint voice of the current. There was a pause before a man's voice spoke.

'Diana. Can you hear me? It's Geoffrey. Listen. Listen to what I'm saying.' The voice paused. Booth pressed the receiver tighter against his ear so as not to miss a word. He knew Geoffrey Stewart's voice well enough to have recognised it at once. The man seemed to be speaking with something of an effort. 'You've got to . . . identify the body. They've got to think it's . . . me. Do you understand?'

'All too bloody well,' Booth muttered under his breath.

'I'll phone you again tomorrow morning at twelve o'clock,' Stewart said and rang off.

Thoughtfully Booth replaced his own receiver. He pushed his chair back and opened the door of the small office. He waited while one of the typists minced past with a sheaf of typewritten statements in her hand. The light outside Clay's office glowed warningly to show that he was not to be disturbed. Beyond, in the big main C.I.D. office, half a dozen officers were at their tables sweating it out like students grappling with their final examinations.

Without even knocking Booth opened the door of Clay's office and went in. The inspector was just rewinding a spool on a small but very modern tape-recorder. At least a dozen spools of tape were stacked on the desk in front of him. On the other table was a cardboard carton bearing the trade name Chocopops and a dozen smaller and more highly coloured cardboard packs with the same inscription. The tape-recording spools had fitted into them almost exactly.

'Well?' Clay enquired, glancing up. 'How did it sound over the phone?'

'You'd have fooled me,' Booth admitted.

'So now we understand why Mrs Stewart thought it was her husband on the phone.'

'Yes, but – how did they get a recording like that, sir?'

'A good recording engineer can take sentences, even single words, from half a dozen tapes and string them together. You can't even detect the breaks. That's why the courts are so reluctant to accept tape-recordings as evidence.'

'I see.'

Clay had finished unwinding the tape. He stopped the machine, removed the spool and placed it carefully in one of the cartons which had been specially marked for identification. It had taken the technical experts twelve hours to monitor the cache of tapes which Booth's team of searchers had eventually found concealed amongst the stock in Kitty Tracy's sweet shop.

Booth moved round to the chair behind the spare table. 'I'm afraid there's still one or two points I'm not clear about, sir.'

'Let me put you in the picture, Sar'nt. As you know, D.C. Griffin has been monitoring these spools which you people found at Kitty Tracy's. Every one of them, except this beauty we've just been listening to, is a recording of a private conversation. Geoffrey Stewart with his wife, Mark Paxton with Mrs Stewart and so on. Someone, and it obviously wasn't just Miss Tracy, went to great lengths to get these recordings. I'm sure I don't have to tell you why.'

'Blackmail?'

'Exactly. Now, in my opinion Kitty Tracy and her partner – Let's give him a name for the time being—'

'Ned Tallboys,' Booth said, before Clay had time to make any suggestion.

Clay shot him a surprised and slightly amused glance.

'Yes, all right, Sar'nt. Let's call him Ned Tallboys. Kitty Tracy and Tallboys discovered that Mrs Stewart and Mark Paxton were having an affair and planned to murder Geoffrey Stewart. They let the plan go through for the simple reason that at a later date they—'

'Intended to blackmail Mrs Stewart.' Once again Booth cut in to show that he possessed powers of deduction of his own.

'Right.' Clay was systematically replacing the remaining spools in their cardboard containers and packing them neatly in the carton. 'Unfortunately for Ned Tallboys, at this point a friend of Kitty Tracy's called Ken Harding came into the picture. Harding knew what they were up to and threatened to go to the police unless he was cut in on the deal. Tallboys agreed to this but after a time he became suspicious. He thought Tracy and Harding were ganging up on him. So he decided that the only thing to do was to get rid of Harding. He murdered him, dressed him up in Geoffrey's Stewart's clothes and took the body out to Benchley Wood. Then by means of this fake telephone call, he persuaded Mrs Stewart to identify the body as her husband's.'

Booth had been watching Clay's neat and competent hands as they slipped the spools into their cartons and closed the flaps. The inspector seemed to be a past-master at turning confusion into a set of neat packages, with apparently disconnected facts sorted out and tucked into their respective pigeon-holes.

'But why should he have wanted to do that?'

'If you committed a murder, what would be your number one problem?'

'Getting rid of the body.'

'Precisely. And the moment Diana Stewart identified the dead man as her husband, Tallboys had in fact solved the problem.'

'I see what you mean. He was banking on the fact that it might be months, years in fact, before Stewart was found.'

'Yes.' Clay placed the last of the spools in the big carton and stood up to carry it over to the top of his filing cabinet. 'And in any case it was not he who murdered Stewart, remember. He had nothing to worry about so far as that murder was concerned.'

'Yes, of course.' Booth's stomach shook as he gave vent to a wheezy chuckle. 'Well, we certainly seemed to have pinned it on poor old Tallboys.'

'Except,' Clay pointed out drily, 'that there is not a shred of evidence to point to Ned Tallboys.'

Someone had been discreetly knocking on the door for a few seconds. Clay pressed a button on his desk to change the illuminated sign on the wall outside. The uniformed clerk who was on duty at the public enquiry desk down below came into the room.

'What is it, Miller?'

'There's a Mr Walter Bowen down below, sir. He'd like to have a word with you.'

Clay looked speculatively at Booth before answering. 'Yes. All right. You can bring him up.'

The door closed on Miller. Clay put the spool with the faked telephone call on it into the drawer of his desk.

Booth was still ruminating on what the inspector had told

him. 'Inspector, when did you first realise that Mark Paxton was having an affair with Mrs Stewart?'

'I had a hunch about it early on. They are really a pretty transparent couple. Then one day—' Clay smiled with amusement at the recollection. 'One day I dropped in unexpectedly on Paxton. Apart from spotting a cigarette she'd been smoking, I saw her handbag on the settee. Paxton threw a newspaper over it, but he was a bit late.'

Clay had tidied away any papers or exhibits that were not for public scrutiny and was again ensconced behind his desk when the reception clerk showed Walter Bowen in.

Walter was in a highly nervous state and for once did not seem to have taken much care about his appearance. His usually neat little beard was showing signs of straggling and his hair was untidy. The knot of his spotted tie was askew and he had buttoned up his check waistcoat wrongly.

'It's very good of you to see me, Inspector,' he began with a hint of obsequiousness. Then he saw Booth looming behind his shoulder and gave a start. 'Oh – good morning, Sergeant.'

'Good morning, sir,' Booth replied gravely, pushing forward the spare chair on which he had been sitting.

Clay waved a hand at the chair. 'Do sit down, Mr Bowen.'

'Thank you.'

Walter sat down, nervously took out his cigarette case, then thought better of it and put the case back in his pocket. He seemed as unhappy as a ninth-wicket batsman facing a spin bowler with the wicket-keeper crouched behind the stumps.

'What can I do for you, sir?' Clay enquired with his usual politeness.

'Well – frankly I don't know that you can do anything, Inspector. It's just that I'm rather worried about my wife.'

'In what way are you worried about Mrs Bowen, sir?'

'She was a friend or rather an acquaintance of—' Walter jerked his head round towards Booth, then brought out a handkerchief and dabbed his brow. 'Look, Inspector, I think I'd better come straight to the point.'

Clay smiled thinly. 'It might be a good idea, sir.'

'Miss Tracy was blackmailing my wife. Thelma used to go to her shop once every month. She – she went there the night Miss Tracy was murdered.'

Booth's shoes creaked as he shifted his weight. Clay's face did not move a muscle.

'Go on, sir,' he said calmly.

'Well, that's it. That's what I came to see you about.'

'It's an interesting piece of information, sir, but I would have preferred to have received it at first hand.'

'I don't understand what you mean.'

'Why didn't your wife tell me about this?'

'She's frightened. And besides—'

'Go on, sir.'

Walter recrossed his legs. His restless eyes switched away from the inspector's steady gaze, darted about the room and eventually found comfort in the sky outside the window. 'My wife and I have had a row. As a matter of fact we've split up – for the time being, at any rate.'

'I'm sorry to hear that.'

'It's just one of those things.' Walter shrugged in an attempt to show that he did not really care, but there was moisture in his foxy eyes. 'It was inevitable, I suppose.'

'Does your wife know that you've come here this morning, Mr Bowen?'

'No. She doesn't.' Walter dragged his eyes back into the room and half turned towards Booth as if hoping to find an ally there. 'That's what our row was about. I told her you were bound to find out about her visit to Miss Tracy and if she didn't come forward now she would probably be suspected of the murder. She just wouldn't listen to me.'

Walter shook his head sadly. Clay did not tell him that he already had evidence of Thelma Bowen's presence in Kitty Tracy's shop on the evening of the murder.

He said: 'What was Miss Tracy blackmailing your wife about, do you know?'

'No. No, I'm afraid I don't.'

'You say your wife went to see Miss Tracy on Wednesday night?'

'Yes. She had an appointment with her at half past six. She was late getting away from the shop and it was a quarter to seven before she rushed off. About half an hour later she returned. She was in a dreadful state, dazed and frightened. I asked her what had happened but she either couldn't or wouldn't tell me. She was almost hysterical. Next morning when I read about the murder I questioned her again. She said that when she arrived at the shop the murder had – well, already happened.'

'You mean, she saw the body?'

'I don't know whether she actually saw the body. She flew into a panic and rushed home.'

'I see.' Suddenly brisk and impersonal, Clay pushed his chair back and stood up.

'Well, thank you, Mr Bowen. You've been most helpful.'

Walter did not stand up for a moment, although Booth already had a hand on the door. He seemed surprised that the interview was ending so abruptly.

'Inspector. If you talk to my wife about this I'd be awfully grateful if you'd—' He stood up and suddenly his manner changed. 'Oh, what the hell!'

'We shall be discreet, sir,' Clay said, proffering his hand with a reassuring smile. 'There's no reason why Mrs Bowen should know that you've been here.'

Walter nodded gratefully and turned to make his exit. Holding the door open for him, Booth asked: 'Where can we get in touch with you, Mr Bowen, if we want to have another chat?'

'Oh—' Walter stopped, a little taken aback by Booth's innocently worded query. 'I've taken a job, a temporary job anyway. Do you know Clayton's, the bookshop at Oldfield?'

Booth nodded.

'I shall be there for the next two or three weeks.'

'Thank you, sir.'

Booth closed the door carefully on Walter. Clay had gone to the window and was staring contemplatively at the buds on the ash tree outside. He had brought his pipe and pouch from his pocket and was unhurriedly thumbing tobacco into the bowl. Booth stared at the back of his neat head. He often wished that he could divine what was going on inside that enigmatic brain.

The weather had taken a turn for the worse in the early afternoon. It seemed that the all too brief spell of sunshine had ended. A sullen layer of grey clouds had lumbered in from the Atlantic and was gradually swathing the whole of southern England in sleety, driving rain. Mark reached Paddock Grange a little before the first downpour came.

He was kept standing outside the front door for much longer than ever before. He had rung the bell twice and knocked three times before Mrs Houston finally appeared. She was wearing a belted woollen coat of severe cut and an uncompromising hat which looked as if it had seen two world wars.

'Oh, Mr Paxton. It's you. I'm sorry to have kept you waiting, but I was upstairs getting ready to go out.'

'Yes, of course, it's your afternoon off, isn't it?' Mark said. He had already stepped past her into the hall.

'I'm just popping across to Oakfield to see my married sister. They've moved into a new house and I've promised to give her a hand. I'll be back in time to get the dinner. I don't like to leave Mrs Stewart too long. I'm worried about her, Mr Paxton. She's been trying to get hold of you, sir. She telephoned your office three times.'

'Yes, I know,' Mark said easily. 'I've been out most of the day.'

During the housekeeper's monologue he had walked along the hall, heading with confident familiarity for the drawing room.

'Mrs Stewart's closed the drawing room up, sir. I've had to put sheets on all the furniture.'

'Oh?' Mark stopped in surprise, his fingers already on the handle.

At that moment Diana appeared at the head of the stairs and began to come slowly down. She was very pale and the shadows under her eyes had deepened, but she was absolutely composed. She was carrying a shiny black handbag over her arm.

Ignoring Mark she spoke to the housekeeper. 'I thought you'd gone, Mrs Houston.'

'Just on my way, madam. I met Mr Paxton on the doorstep.'

'Give your sister my regards and tell her I hope she likes her new house.'

'Yes. I will. And leave the dinner to me, mind. I'll be back in time to put it in the oven for you.'

Diana nodded listlessly and stood watching Mrs Houston till she had let herself out through the front door. Only then did she swing her eyes to Mark.

'Hello, Mark.'

'Hello. Can we go somewhere and talk? What's the idea of closing the drawing room up?'

'That room gives me the shivers. I couldn't bear to be in it any longer. We can go into my office. Geoffrey used to call it the hell-hole.'

She crossed the hall and opened the door to a small room which opened out on to the rose-garden at the side of the house. It was a bright and colourful room, part office, part sewing room, part sitting room and was in a state of what could only be called organised confusion. Papers lay in little bundles all over the desk and there were bits of clothing and sewing draped over the chairs.

Diana led him into the room and placed her handbag on an antique sewing table.

He said 'You look tired.'

'I didn't have a very good night.' She still kept her back to him as she moved a pinned-together dress from the arm of the chair. 'I've been trying to get you on the phone. I've been trying the whole morning.'

'Yes, I know. I'm sorry, darling, but I had two important appointments.'

He moved up behind her and put his hands on her upper arms. When he tried to turn her round so that they could kiss she twisted away from him.

'What happened last night?'

Unabashed by the rebuff, Mark sat down on the arm of the chair. He seemed very pleased with events and only anxious to share his good news with her.

'I've got quite a lot to tell you. I saw that girl, Diana Valesco. We had a long talk and—'

'What's she like?' Diana cut in with urgent intensity.

Mark hesitated. 'Do you want me to be frank?'

'Of course I want you to be frank!' she snapped out, rounding on him. 'For God's sake, why would I ask you if I didn't want you to—'

'Diana, what is it? What's the matter?' He stood up and again tried to take her in his arms, but again she evaded him and went over to the window. The first heavy spots of rain were spattering against the glass.

'Tell me about this girl.'

'She's Italian,' Mark said slowly. 'Dark and – er – very well proportioned. A real good-looker. It's obvious why Geoffrey had fallen so much in love with her.'

'How do you know?' she challenged him bitterly. 'How do you know he was in love with her?'

'Diana, what's the matter with you?' Mark's anger showed through the careful suavity of his manner. 'Do you want to know the truth? Do you want to know what happened last night, or don't you?'

She turned and for a moment just stared at him. Her eyes were hostile, her nose pinched in, her mouth a thin line. She gave him a little nod. 'Go on.'

'It appears Geoffrey met her about six months ago.' Mark moved towards the mock-Adam fireplace and leant an elbow on the mantelpiece. 'They bumped into each other in Chelsea. I mean literally bumped into each other. Geoffrey was crossing the road and she was running for a taxi when, wham!' Mark banged a fist into the palm of his hand. 'She hurt her foot pretty badly so he put her into the cab and took her home. That's how it started.'

'Who came like a bat out of hell.' Diana repeated the inscription from the cigarette case with angry sarcasm.

Mark nodded. 'He used the phrase when she bumped into him and she just didn't understand it. Later, when they got to know each other, she asked him what it meant. He tried to explain. He even tried to translate it into Italian for her, but it was impossible. It became a little joke between them.'

'A rather costly little joke, I should imagine, so far as Geoffrey was concerned.'

'I think you're wrong about her, darling. It's my impression this girl's had very little out of him. She didn't even know about the will until – I told her.'

Diana noted his hesitation. 'I find that very difficult to believe.'

'It's true.'

'Well, what happened when you did tell her?'

Mark detached himself from the mantelpiece and once again tried to make an approach to her. It was evident that affectionate physical contact was going to be needed to help him put over the point he was about to make.

'She's worried. She's frightened you're going to contest the will.'

'I am going to!'

She was as nervous of his touch as if they were strangers. He had to approach her as cautiously as a schoolboy making an opening pass at his first girl-friend.

'Diana, listen. I've had a talk to this girl. She's not what you think she is. At the moment she's hard up and—'

'What do you mean – hard up! For God's sake!'

'Darling, if you contest the will it'll be months, years perhaps before anyone gets a bob out of anything.'

'That's not what you said yesterday,' Diana pointed out, withdrawing her hand from his.

'I know. I know what I said yesterday, but that was before

I saw this girl. Diana, she's prepared to do a deal with you. She's told me, quite frankly, if you can let her have ten thousand pounds now – straight away—'

Mark stopped abruptly. Diana had moved away from him and was fingering the handbag on the sewing table. Now she turned round swiftly and he saw an expression of suspicion in her eyes which had never been there before.

Very quietly she said: 'You must want me to give you ten thousand pounds?'

'Not me!' he protested, with an exaggerated gesture of the hand. 'This girl. Diana darling, don't you understand what I'm talking about?'

For answer Diana snapped open the catch of her handbag. She drew out an envelope and threw it down on to the seat of the armchair.

'Read that letter. I received it this morning.'

'What is it?'

'Read it!'

Her tone had hardened. Mark's brow furrowed. He stooped to pick up the envelope. Moving away towards the window he pulled the sheet of notepaper out. He knew she was studying every change of expression. Pretending that he needed the light from the window to read the message he kept his face averted.

The message had been printed on unheaded paper with a ball-point pen.

THOUGHT YOU MIGHT LIKE TO KNOW
MARK PAXTON LEAVES FOR SYDNEY ON
MONDAY. B.O.A.C. FLIGHT 203.

He read the letter through twice then spun round angrily. 'What the hell does this mean?'

The question trailed off on his lips. Diana had taken a small automatic from her handbag. She was gripping it tightly in her hand and the barrel, trembling a little, was aimed waveringly at his chest.

'Don't you know what it means, Mark?'

'No, I'm damned if I do! Diana, don't be an idiot. Put that thing away.' He was watching her eyes, looking for the ruthless hatred which she would need to press the trigger. He could only see an immeasurable sadness. 'Good God, do you think I'd walk out on you at a time like this?'

'Yes, I do.' She took a pace forward, so that the sewing table was no longer between them. 'You are walking out on me. That's why you wanted ten thousand pounds, not because that girl asked you to—'

'Diana, for heaven's sake!' Mark tried to laugh, recover his confident charm, ridicule her notion. 'Some little bastard sends you an anonymous letter and you're immediately ready to believe I'm walking out on you.'

She shook her head. 'It's no use, Mark.'

'What do you mean?'

'I checked with B.O.A.C. I phoned them the moment I got this letter.'

A sudden flurry of wind dashed raindrops against the window pane. It sounded almost as if someone had thrown a handful of tiny pebbles against the glass.

'Yes, well—' Mark fumbled for ideas, his gaze riveted to the barrel of the automatic. For the first time there was a hint of panic in his voice. 'Look, Diana, I can explain. I can explain about B.O.A.C. Someone at the office asked me to make a reservation for them and naturally—'

'You're lying!' Diana's statement carried the sting of a whiplash. 'All along you've been lying. You've been lying every time you told me you loved me. I was blind to it till yesterday, but I felt the change in you when you heard that Geoffrey's money was not coming to me—'

'I'm not lying. Honestly, darling, I—'

'You've called me darling for the last time, Mark.'

Unobtrusively he had been working his way closer to her as they talked. His eyes rose from the automatic to meet hers. Always he had had the power to bend her to his will and he was confident that he could do so now. Moving in, he stretched out a hand.

'Give me that gun, Diana.'

He saw her eyes dilate and knew that he had the mastery of her, but as his right hand clamped on hers and his left came up to twist the automatic from her grasp, her fingers contracted involuntarily. The gun leapt with the explosion.

Mark stiffened. His hands clutched at his chest. His eyes glazed. With a gasp he fell sideways on to the arm of the chair, then rolled off it on to the floor.

Horrified at what she had done Diana stood transfixed, watching his writhing body. Then, dropping the gun she rushed towards him and knelt down beside him, cradling his head with her hands, sobbing and pleading.

'Mark, darling. I didn't mean to do it. I didn't mean to hurt you, darling! Mark!'

In less than a minute she realised that it was no use; the bullet had penetrated his heart.

She straightened up slowly, wondering why she didn't collapse into a screaming hysteria, why she felt this icy calmness and sense of liberation. It was almost as if she had been through this scene in rehearsal and knew exactly what to do next.

She took a length of dress material and stretched it over the still figure on the floor, then she stood for a few moments looking at the rain streaming down the panes of the French windows. Finally she went to the untidy writing desk where she always did her household accounts and picked up the telephone receiver. She dialled a number. Without delay a crisp, business-like voice answered her.

'Alunbury police.'

'This is Mrs Stewart. Mrs Geoffrey Stewart. I—'

Her voice failed momentarily.

'Yes, Mrs Stewart,' the police clerk prompted.

'I want to speak to Inspector Clay, please.'

The newspaper editors had really gone to town on the latest Alunbury shooting. The Saturday morning editions carried photographs of Diana, Mark and Paddock Grange. The tragedy seemed to have all the ingredients of a first class *crime passionel.* Mrs Houston had been in great demand for cosy side lights on the relationship of the couple, or glimpses of intimate scenes through key-holes. Schooled by Clay she had kept her loyal mouth tight and shut and refused to make any comment whatsoever. Which only inspired the reporters working on the job to draw more fully on their own imagination.

Ned Tallboys had sent Vince to purchase a copy of every paper he could lay his hands on. He had them spread out on the desk of the glass-fronted office at the back of the showroom. He was leaning back in his chair with one leg supported on an open drawer of the desk, the *Daily Mail* opened in front of his face. So he did not see Clay pull his car on to the forecourt and, following Vince's directions, walk into the showroom.

Passing the Maserati, Clay noticed that its price had been slashed by £500. He glanced quickly at the other models and saw that they had all been reduced by substantial amounts. Perhaps, after all, something here might be within his reach . . . He quickly banished the tempting thought and moved on towards the office. Ned Tallboys had heard the echoing footsteps and lowered his paper. He was on his feet with a salesman's smile of welcome by the time Clay pushed open the door.

'Good morning, Inspector. Can I interest you in a motor-car?'

'I see you've reduced your prices, sir.'

'Yes. Sales have been a bit sticky lately and I've decided to accept lower profit margins in favour of a quicker flow. There are some really good bargains out there now.'

'I'm sure. But I didn't come to discuss buying a new car. I wondered if I might use your phone?'

Ned threw his newspaper down and moved out from behind the desk. 'Yes, of course. Help yourself.'

'I was buying some petrol and suddenly remembered a call I had to make.' Squeezing round to get at the telephone, Clay nodded towards the outspread newspapers. 'That's a terrible business, isn't it, sir?'

'My God, you can say that again!' Ned shook his head with a puzzled frown. 'When I saw the paper this morning I just couldn't believe it. Inspector—'

Clay had sat down in Ned's seat and was pulling the telephone closer. Noticing the garage owner's hesitation he glanced up.

'Yes, sir?'

'I probably ought not to ask you this, but – did you know about Mrs Stewart and Mark Paxton?'

Ned seemed to have trouble in getting the question out.

'I suspected they were more than just friends, if that's what you mean, sir.'

'Do you know, it never crossed my mind, not for a minute. And yet, now you come to think of it, he was a good-looking chap and they were always together.' Ned flicked a speck from the lapel of his tweed jacket and grinned wryly. 'I'm beginning to think I'm a bit of a dimwit.'

'I wouldn't say that, sir,' Clay assured him seriously. 'You just haven't got a suspicious nature.'

'But that's just it. I have! As a rule I'd suspect my own grandmother.'

Clay smiled and lifted the receiver, preparatory to dialling.

'How did the row start, Inspector? I mean, what triggered it off?'

'A letter, sir.'

'A letter?'

Clay deliberately replaced the receiver and reached into his inside pocket. He produced an envelope and handed it to Ned. Ned extracted the sheet of paper and frowned over it. Outside on the forecourt Vince had finished filling up Clay's car and was pushing it away from the front of the pumps to make way for an incoming driver.

'Is this the actual letter?' Ned was asking.

'Yes.'

'You mean—' Ned looked disbelievingly at the paper in his hand. 'She killed him just because of this.'

'She didn't mean to kill him, sir. The gun went off accidentally.' Clay took the letter from Ned as he spoke, replaced it in the envelope and put it back in his pocket. 'But I see what you mean. As soon as Mrs Stewart received this letter she telephoned B.O.A.C.'

'And he'd made a booking?'

'Yes. He'd made a booking, all right. He was flying to Sydney on Monday afternoon.'

'The little bastard,' Ned said with quiet venom. 'Walking out on her like that.'

Clay nodded his agreement. His hand was once more on the telephone. 'Now, sir, if you don't mind.'

'Yes, of course. I'm sorry. Please go ahead.'

Ned began to move towards the door.

'I'm only ringing the office, sir. It's not private.'

'It's about time I did some work anyway—'

Ned drifted out. Clay dialled his number, his eyes following the other man as it rang.

'Alunbury police.'

'Clay here. Put me through to Sergeant Booth, please.'

While he waited, Clay's eyes prowled methodically over Tallboys' desk, subconsciously making an inventory of everything they saw there.

'Inspector? Sergeant Booth's not here. He went over to Oakfield about an hour ago.'

'That's Dawson, isn't it?'

'Yes, sir.'

'It's all right, Dawson. Nothing that can't wait.'

'Don't ring off, sir,' Dawson said quickly. 'There's a Mrs Bowen here, waiting to see you. She says it's urgent.'

'Mrs Bowen?' Clay reflected for a moment, then made up his mind. 'All right. Keep her there. I'll be back in about fifteen minutes.'

'Mrs Bowen, I appreciate that Diana Stewart is a friend of yours, but I'm sure you didn't come here just to talk about her and Mark Paxton.'

Startled by the sharp tone Thelma Bowen halted in the midst of her non-stop monologue. She gaped at Clay, her jaw dropping like someone with hysteria who has had a sharp smack on the face. Clay had found her in the C.I.D. waiting room, chewing her handkerchief. She was clad carelessly in dowdy clothes and, without her make-up, looked a good ten years older than the Thelma who usually presented herself to the world. Knowing human nature, Clay had given her her head for a few minutes before cracking the whip.

'No. No I didn't.'

'What is it you want to tell me?'

'Well, I . . .'

Thelma had gone now to the other extreme and seemed unable to find the words she wanted.

'Go on.'

'I wanted to talk to you about Kitty Tracy,' she jerked out, still hesitating. 'About what happened the other night she – the night she was murdered.'

'I was hoping you'd come to that. Go ahead, Mrs Bowen.'

Thelma took a deep breath. 'About two years ago I bought some jewellery from a man called Ken Harding. It had been stolen – I knew it was stolen at the time but like a fool I – I sold it to a customer of mine. Six months later Ken offered me some more jewellery and I did the same thing again. After that we did quite a few deals together.'

'You were receiving stolen property,' Clay commented, to put the record straight.

Thelma nodded submissively. 'Then one night Kitty Tracy rang me up. She didn't say exactly what she wanted, but she mentioned Ken Harding's name and she hinted that she knew what was going on.'

'That was her technique, I'm afraid. First to make you curious, whether she made sense or not, then to scare the hell out of you.'

'About a fortnight after her phone call she asked me to call round and see her.' Thelma stared out of the window, the corners of her mouth drooping. 'I've been calling round to see her ever since.'

'How much did she get out of you?'

'Two hundred pounds in cash, every month. You see, she had some papers I'd signed – papers I'd given to Ken Harding when – when we were fixing up—'

Thelma sniffed and blew her nose on a tiny handkerchief which seemed ridiculous in her man-sized hand.

Clay prompted quietly: 'Tell me about Wednesday night, Mrs Bowen.'

'I went there at about seven.' She squared her shoulders, determined to reconstruct the scene for Clay without hysteria. 'I used to walk into the shop and then go straight upstairs. She was usually sitting in her chair waiting for me. On Wednesday when I got to the door of her sitting room I realised that she wasn't there and that the place had been ransacked. I was looking at the incredible disorder when I heard a step on the landing behind me. I knew someone must have come out of the bedroom but before I could turn round I received a terrible blow on the head. It knocked me clean out.'

'You didn't see this person at all? Could you tell if it was a man or a woman?'

'I feel sure it was a man. Something about the footsteps and the force of that blow. I must have been out for about ten minutes. When I came round I was lying sprawled at the top of the stairs. I remembered the state the sitting room had been in. I was sure something awful had happened and I – I just ran out of the shop and went home.'

'Didn't you look for Miss Tracy? Didn't you go into the bedroom?'

'No. I didn't. I was feeling dreadful. Whatever had happened I didn't want to get involved in it.'

Clay stood up and went to open the window a few more inches. Tiny beads of perspiration were forming on Thelma's brow. He returned and sat down on the edge of his desk. In that position he looked somehow less formidable.

'Mrs Bowen, you say Kitty Tracy was blackmailing you and that you paid her two hundred pounds a month. Was it always just a question of money? Didn't she sometimes ask you to do things for her?'

'Yes, she did.' Thelma looked at Clay gratefully. She had been dreading this confession but now that the worst of it was over, she was beginning to feel better. 'She made me lie to Diana about that phone call. There wasn't a phone call, of course. Geoffrey was already dead.'

Clay nodded. 'She wanted Mrs Stewart to go to the motel and identify the body.'

'Yes, but why? I never understood why.'

The inspector moved back to the chair behind his desk and sat down again.

'Mrs Bowen, I'm going to tell you something about Kitty Tracy, something you don't know. Although she was blackmailing you, Tracy actually worked for a man called— Well, let's call him Smith for the time being. Smith was the real blackmailer, he really ran the racket. One day Kitty Tracy and your friend Ken Harding decided to start up on their own. It's my bet you were the first victim. Smith took a long time to discover what was happening, but when he did he completely lost control of his temper. He beat Harding to death and tried to cover the murder up—'

'By passing off Ken Harding as Geoffrey Stewart.'

'Right. But Kitty Tracy had been fond of Ken Harding and she made up her mind not to let Smith get away with it. She knew that once we—'

'Once you found the body of Geoffrey Stewart you'd become curious about the other body, the one at Benchley Wood.'

'Right again, Mrs Bowen.' Clay contemplated Thelma approvingly. She had perked up in the last few minutes and was entering with enthusiasm into the spirit of the thing.

'And it was Smith who murdered Kitty?'

'Yes. He was obviously searching for something when you disturbed him. And I think I know what he was searching for.'

'You mean—?' Thelma hesitated to commit herself. Her new-found confidence evaporated suddenly and her cheeks began to tremble again.

'I don't want to frighten you, Mrs Bowen,' Clay said slowly. 'But – my bet is you'll be hearing from Mr Smith.'

Thelma did not have to wait long. She did a good afternoon's business on Saturday afternoon. Chatting up her customers – legitimate ones, this time – had taken her mind off Clay's warning. She had literally to ask the last customer to leave in order to put the shutters up reasonably soon after half past five. Margery, she knew, had a date with her young man and was like a cat on hot bricks to get away.

'All right, Margery,' she said, as the customer finally departed. 'You run along. I'll see to everything and lock up.'

'Oh, thank you, Mrs Bowen.'

Margery did not need telling twice. She ran to collect her raincoat and a minute later was hurrying out into the street.

Thelma saw her go up to a tall, fair young man who was standing beside a spanking new Honda 250, which he had pulled up on to its stand. His crash helmet had been laid on the riding seat.

Wincing at the thought of her treasured assistant on the pillion of the scarlet machine, Thelma turned away and started switching the lights off. She emptied the till and put the day's takings in the brand new Chubb safe which she had recently had installed in her office. She made doubly certain that it was well and truly locked up before leaving. For her less respectable transactions, Thelma could not rely on banks and, as she usually dealt in cash, she had decided to provide her own vault.

A few minutes later she was padlocking the grill which closed across the front of Limelight Ltd. She put the keys in her handbag and was turning to make her way home when a car, which had been parked for some time a little way down the street, slid forward and stopped beside her. The driver opened his door and came round the back of the car towards her. She glanced up and saw the worried face of Walter.

'Hello,' she said uncompromisingly. 'What are you doing here?'

'I should have thought that was obvious, Thelma. I've been waiting for you.'

'Look, Walter, I told you yesterday I haven't the slightest intention of—'

She was turning away, but Walter took hold of her arm. 'Thelma, listen. I've got to talk to you.'

'It's no use, Walter,' she retorted, shaking him off. 'I'm not lending you another bob.'

'Thelma, listen to me!' Walter insisted. 'It's important! I've got a message for you. It's about Kitty Tracy.'

Thelma froze. 'What do you mean – about Kitty Tracy?'

'Someone telephoned me at the bookshop. I don't know who it was, but—' Walter flung a glance up and down the pavement. 'Look, for God's sake get into the car. We can't talk here.'

Without further comment Thelma opened the passenger's door and inserted herself into the rather inadequate space. Walter got into the driving seat and with fussy incompetence coaxed the car out into the stream of evening traffic.

'Now, what's all this?' Thelma demanded.

'It happened at lunch time. I was on my own.' Walter gave his account in disjointed phrases, half his attention on the hazards of Alunbury's rush hour. 'Clayton had gone to the bank and I was sorting through some of the paperbacks. The phone rang and when I answered it a man's voice said: "Is that Walter Bowen?" When I told him it was he said: "I've got a message for your wife, Mr. Bowen. Tell her I've got the papers Kitty Tracy had. Tell her that I'm prepared to do a deal. Five thousand pounds in cash. I'll phone you again tomorrow."'

'That's all?'

'Yes. That's all he said.'

'And you didn't recognise his voice?'

'No. I didn't.' Walter took his eyes off the road for long enough to shoot her a worried glance. 'Thelma, what was he talking about?'

Thelma ignored the question. 'Walter, I want you to do something for me. When he rings tomorrow tell him I'll see him on Monday afternoon at Paddock Grange.'

'Paddock Grange? The Stewart place?'

'Yes.'

'But why Paddock Grange?'

'Tell him to be in the drawing room at two o'clock. I'll bring the money with me. Five thousand pounds in cash.'

'Yes, all right,' Walter agreed, completely mystified. Suddenly he put on the brakes and pulled in to the side of the road. He looked at her with an expression of such genuine concern that the hostile line of her mouth softened. 'Thelma, I hope to God you know what you're doing.'

The roses were in full bloom at Paddock Grange. Monday was one of those perfect late summer days when the birds chorus their rapture from dawn to dusk and by the middle of the day the temperature was in the seventies.

Briefed by Booth, Mrs Houston had departed at mid-morning to the house of her younger sister at Oakfield. Both front and back door had been left unlocked. During the lunch break Paddock Grange was left to ruminate in peace on the series of events which had taken place in the past week. Clay had given strict instructions that the police net was not to close in until *after* Thelma had gone up to the house. There was no way of knowing how 'Mr Smith' intended to approach the place and Clay did not want him bumping into some constable hiding amongst the shrubs at the back of the house. He had assured Thelma that she was running no real risk, and had given her a promise that he would make certain that she had got clear before giving the signal for the cordon to close in. Thereafter half a dozen police cars and a score of police officers would put a strangle-hold on Paddock Grange which would make it impossible for the quarry to escape.

A few minutes before two o'clock Clay and Booth were quietly dropped by one of the C.I.D. cars at a side entrance to Paddock Grange. They made their way along a leaf-strewn path towards the front of the house.

'I wonder who'll take this place over now,' Booth murmured. 'Even if she gets off with a light sentence, Mrs Stewart will hardly want to come back here.'

Clay was amused by the sympathetic tone in Booth's voice. 'You've been to see her, then?'

'Yes,' Booth admitted gruffly. 'I saw her just for a few minutes.'

'How is she?'

'She's upset because they've refused bail, of course, but if you ask me she's taking it pretty well. You know, it's a funny thing, but I almost feel sorry for that woman.'

'Then remind me to keep you off the jury, Booth,' Clay said, holding a branch to prevent it whipping back into the sergeant's face.

'Oh I know, strictly speaking she's a bad lot.'

'Strictly speaking you're a sucker, and if you'd been married to her you'd have been a dead sucker by now.'

Through the trees the house had come into view. The two men fell silent and stepped off the path on to grass to deaden their footsteps. They used the cover of the trees to get behind a screen of bushes from which they could command a view of the front of the house. It was one minute to two. Crouching,

Clay stared at the windows, half expecting to see the blur of a face at one of them. He could not help feeling a thrill of excitement at the knowledge that, if his plan worked, the man he had been hunting for a week was waiting for him behind the elegant Georgian façade.

He took the pocket radio out, extended the aerial, gave the call sign and said:

'Clay here. We're in position. Get set, it will be any minute now.'

Just as he finished speaking, Thelma's car could be heard coming up the drive. She was moving slowly so as to be sure she arrived at the house exactly at two. Clay had impressed on her the importance of split-second timing. She stopped the car in front of the house and switched off the engine.

In the silence the sound of the town hall clock in Alunbury striking the hour drifted faintly across the sunlit fields. Thelma got out of the car. She was carrying her most voluminous handbag. She looked tense and nervous but quite determined. She went up the stairs of the front entrance and disappeared inside the house.

This was the moment Clay feared most. Despite his assurances to Thelma he had to admit that there was a big element of risk in allowing her to face 'Mr Smith' alone. All he had asked her to do was hand over the money and then get out. If she wasn't out in three minutes, then he and Booth were going in.

The red indicator seemed to crawl round the face of Clay's watch. In the distance a train clattered into Alunbury station, the tempo of its wheel-patter gradually slowing. Clay's ears were stretched for the sound he dreaded most. A shot from inside the house.

The hand completed its third sweep. Clay straightened up. He pulled the aerial of the radio set out again. But Booth already had a hand on his arm.

'She's coming out.'

Thelma's face showed that she had been through an ordeal. She stumbled and nearly fell on the steps. Then she recovered herself and made for her car. As soon as the engine had started and she was moving away down the drive, Clay activated his radio.

'Greenlight,' he said crisply. 'Close in now.'

He put the set away and with Booth at his shoulder marched briskly across the front drive. Before they even reached the door, a couple of motor-cycle police had turned into the avenue and were speeding up to the house.

Clay knew that Booth had drawn a gun and was covering him as he quickly walked down the hall and pushed open the door of the drawing room.

Walter Bowen was sitting in the sheeted armchair in front of the fireplace. Clay stared at him and at the ghostly room with its shrouded tables and chairs. Booth could tell that for once the inspector was completely bowled over with astonishment.

'Where's the money?' he demanded.

Walter recrossed his legs and licked his lips.

'I don't know anything about any money,' he said.

Clay reached him in three quick strides, grabbed him by the coat lapels and hauled him to his feet.

'Then what the hell are you doing here?'

The force of Clay's anger shook Walter. His eyes were nearly popping out of his head.

'I wanted to make sure nothing happened to Thelma,' he gasped. 'I knew you were using her as a decoy—'

'What's happened to the money?' Clay said again. 'Who was here besides you and Mrs Bowen?'

'No one.' Walter tried to pull Clay's hands away from their choking grip. 'She's taken the money with her.'

'WHAT! Where to?'

'I – I don't know,' Walter whispered.

Clay glared into his eyes, then flung him down into the chair. All the old calmness and courtesy had vanished.

'You know but you're not telling,' he growled. He turned to Booth. 'You can put that gun away. This dog won't bite. I want this room searched, and double quick.'

The two men went round the room, stripping off the sheets, while outside the police net closed in on a cage from which the bird had flown. Clay found the tape-recorder hastily concealed in the corner of the settee. It was the one he had seen on the bench in Ned Tallboys' private office.

He placed it on the table and switched it on. The sound-track was blank. He operated the rewind switch, took the tape back to zero and tried again. This time the recorded message came over loud and clear.

'Good afternoon, Thelma. Sorry not to be here to meet you personally, but I'm not quite sure whether I can trust you and so I prefer to meet you on ground of my own choosing. This time do exactly as I say and make sure you are not followed. Take the money and drive straight to Lyncote Manor. I will be waiting for you there. If you bring the police, Mrs Houston, who is with me, will be shot. I kid you not. Now hide this tape-recorder where our dear friend Clay won't find it and be on your way.'

The message had ended. Clay turned to Booth who had abandoned the search and was standing listening.

'Lyncote Manor! Come on, Booth. We've wasted enough time here.'

Walter struggled to his feet as the two police officers headed for the door.

'He'll do it,' he shouted after them. 'He'll kill Mrs Houston – and maybe Thelma too!'

Clay did not seem to hear. On the steps of the house he paused. The two motor-cycle patrolmen had heaved their machines on to stands and were taking off their gloves. The crew of a Rover police car equipped with blue light, siren, high mounted spot-lights and illuminated sign had dismounted and were chatting to them.

'Nobody came down the front drive, Inspector. He must have headed the other way.'

'I'm taking your car,' Clay told the driver. 'I'll be in touch by radio.'

'But that's against the—'

'I'll be responsible,' Clay snapped. 'Jump in, Booth.'

Clay settled behind the driving wheel and made sure that he had all the pedals and controls within reach. The ignition key was in the socket. He twisted the key and the engine started with an encouraging roar. As Booth slammed the door on the passenger side, he let in the clutch and accelerated down the drive. The crew of the car were left scratching their heads in angry bewilderment.

'She's got a good five minutes start on us,' Clay said. 'Which means she's probably at Lyncote Manor already.'

'You're not afraid he'll carry out his threat if we follow?'

'I'm more afraid of what'll happen if we don't,' Clay said grimly, slowing only slightly to turn out on to the main road. The thought uppermost in his mind was that of all the people involved in this business, Mrs Houston was the most innocent. And Tallboys, with ruthless acumen, had chosen her as hostage.

'You knew it was Tallboys all along?'

'I didn't really know until I showed him that note. I'd made a copy of the note Mrs Stewart received and showed it to him. He fell for it. He said: "Is this the *actual* note, Inspector?" '

'Thus giving away the fact that he knew damn well it wasn't.'

'Exactly. If he hadn't seen the original note he wouldn't have questioned it.'

'What was the point of tipping Mrs Stewart off about the B.O.A.C. booking?'

'Tallboys was jealous of the success Mark Paxton was having with Diana Stewart. He hated his guts. He'd have done anything he could to harm Paxton – and in his way he succeeded.'

There was no more talk between the two men as Clay hustled the Rover towards Lyncote Manor. He was approaching the derelict property by the same route as Geoffrey Stewart had taken on the morning when he had walked to meet his murderer.

Clay had slowed in order to enter the gateway cautiously. He was just about to turn in when an E-type Jaguar burst like a rocket from the driveway. It missed the bonnet of the Rover by a hair's-breadth, skidded into a broadside as its driver wrenched the wheel, and vanished up the Oakfield road with a roar from its exhaust.

'That was Tallboys!' Booth shouted unnecessarily.

'Was he alone?'

'Yes.'

'Call up the station. Tell them to send a car to Lyncote Manor and check that the two women are all right, then warn all cars to be on the look-out for a black Jaguar, E-type, heading west from the Alunbury area.'

While Booth busied himself with the radio controls, Clay quickly turned the car and headed it in the direction Tallboys had gone. He intended to catch him. The E-type was a far faster car than the Rover, but Clay knew that Tallboys was a showy rather than a really quick driver and he believed that he could wear him down. He settled down to drive as he had never driven since he had taken the police driving course.

The Jaguar had already disappeared round the next bend. The road into Oakfield was a rather narrow, winding one. Clay knew that there was a T-junction in the village and he wanted to see which way Tallboys would turn. But he could not catch him on that stretch of road and when the Rover careered between the first of the houses and the T-junction came in sight, there was no sign of the Jaguar.

'Shall I switch the siren on?' Booth shouted above the noise of the engine.

'Not yet. Let's have the blue light, though.'

Tallboys had given himself away by his own untidy and violent driving. Black marks on the tarmac showed where he had braked and then accelerated away from the corner, spinning his rear wheels.

Clay turned left to follow. Half a mile outside the village the road, now a main highway, began to snake over a ridge of hills. Double white lines confined the traffic to two lanes. A heavy lorry was labouring in low gear up the slope and three private cars were blocked behind it. The last of them was the Jaguar. As the Rover came into sight, Tallboys pulled out suicidally and passed the three vehicles in front of him. He made it just before a big pantechnicon came charging down the hill.

'Put the siren on,' Clay commanded. With the awful wailing noise reaching out ahead of them they closed rapidly on the string of cars. Booth closed his eyes as Clay went round the outside of them, his wheels straddling the double white line.

The Jaguar was the only car on the road ahead, but on the up-gradient its power and speed had the measure of the Rover. When Clay topped the rise he could see half a mile of straight road ahead. There was nothing on it except a crawling Mini driven by a grey-haired lady.

Clay settled down to gain ground by sound, fast driving. He surmised that Tallboys would stick to fast main roads where his greater speed would give him the advantage. The next town was five miles ahead.

In that distance they twice spotted the Jaguar as it pulled out to pass slower cars. But always, after these slight checks, it forged away again.

'Trouble is,' Booth reported, 'all available cars were on the Paddock Grange job.'

Clay grunted. He was still sore at the way Tallboys had outsmarted him.

As they approached the town, Booth switched the siren on again. The Jaguar had gained a lot of ground on the long straight section, but the traffic of the little township parted to leave a free passage to the Rover. The flashing blue light and the siren echoing deafeningly from the house fronts brought everything to a stop. Clay dashed through the main street at seventy miles an hour, every nerve tensed to brake if some foolish pedestrian darted out. As they emerged from the built-up area the Jaguar was only two hundred yards away.

Tallboys had realised that there was something odd going on behind him and he had spotted the police car in his mirror. He began now to take suicidal risks, forcing his way past private cars, cutting in between lorry drivers travelling in tandem. Clay stalked him, knowing that sooner or later his chance would come, that Tallboys would make some mistake.

The mistake, when it came, was one of tactics rather than driving. Road signs were indicating that Barchester was seven miles away and the first of the placards advertising the Pine Lodge Motel had flashed past. Perhaps Tallboys regarded this as an evil omen, perhaps he guessed, rightly, that a radio message had gone ahead to Barchester police warning them to set up road blocks.

Whatever the reason he decided to turn off the main road and try to get lost in the countryside. From half a mile behind, Clay saw his brake lights glow as he slowed abruptly. The tail of the Jaguar slewed round as he made the turning on to a minor road that led up into wooded hills.

Twenty seconds later Clay made the same turn and Booth exclaimed with excitement.

'We've got him now!'

A large-lettered sign at the entrance to the turning read: 'Road closed in three miles. Pedestrian traffic only at Marley bridge'.

'I wonder what he'll do,' Clay mused. 'Make a run for it on foot, perhaps. Keep contact with the Barchester police. We may have a manhunt on our hands.'

While Booth conversed with the radio control room at Barchester in that impersonal measured tone which cuts even the most dramatic messages down to banality, Clay concentrated on keeping the car on the narrow road. There was barely room for two vehicles to pass. Ned Tallboys must also have seen the sign at the turning into this road and Clay half expected to round a corner and find the Jaguar abandoned in the middle of the road.

He was quite unprepared for the desperate gamble on which Tallboys staked everything.

The Rover was building speed on one of the rare straight sections when round the bend ahead came the Jaguar, moving full speed in the opposite direction. Tallboys had doubled back on his tracks. Now, instead of braking he was accelerating fiercely.

Clay realised that he was being challenged to one of the tests of nerves which Californian youths are said to indulge in on long, lonely stretches of road. Two vehicles drive towards each other at full speed. The first to turn away is 'chicken'.

Clay had to make an instant decision. If he braked Tallboys could squeeze past him on either side. If he slewed his car across the road a fatal accident was certain. He accepted the challenge and drove straight for the Jaguar, his foot hard down on the accelerator. It all happened in a couple of seconds, the cars converged on each other at a combined speed of a hundred and thirty miles an hour, the long shark-like snout of the Jaguar lancing towards the Rover with its two high-mounted lamps and flashing blue light. At the last moment Tallboys' nerve failed. He pulled his left hand down and took the Jaguar through the hedge and into the field beyond.

As the two police officers ran back they could hear his engine racing as he tried to get some wheel purchase on the ploughed field. They burst through the gap the Jaguar had torn in the hedge to find him struggling free of his safety harness. Thelma Bowen's monster handbag was clutched in his right hand. He seemed miraculously unhurt.

'I think I'll take charge of that, sir,' Clay said quietly, holding out his hand for Thelma's handbag.

Tallboys hesitated, wondering whether he still had a chance to make a dash for it. But Booth, his moustache quivering ominously and his blue eyes blazing, had moved round behind him and deftly removed the revolver from his pocket. Tallboys handed the bag over and stood there with simulated bravado, casually flicking the non-existent spot from the lapel of his jacket. For once he had no bantering talk ready.

The crew of the Barchester police car which came nosing down the lane a few minutes later met them as they emerged through the gap in the hedge, Clay and Booth each holding one of Tallboys' arms. The uniformed men put the handcuffs on Ned and took him away in their car, inside which the radio loudspeaker was still crackling busily.

Hearing his own name mentioned by the impersonal voice, Clay cocked an ear. 'Inform Inspector Clay no casualties at Lyncote Manor. Repeat, no casualties at Lyncote Manor.'

'Lucky for you, Tallboys,' Booth growled as he bundled him into the back seat.

'Where do you want him?' the Barchester driver asked Clay, jerking his head at the prisoner.

'Can you take him back to Alunbury for me? I'd like to charge him there.'

'Right, sir.'

'Before you go,' Clay stopped the driver as he was getting into the car, 'could one of you give us a hand to get this Jaguar back on the road?'

The combined strength of three policemen, two of them fifteen-stoners, soon had the Jaguar back on the road. Apart from a couple of dents in the bodywork and deep scores along the paintwork, she was unharmed. By that time three more police cars had come nosing up the lane, their blue lights winking.

Booth was opening the door on the driver's side of the Jaguar.

'You can leave this to me, sir,' he called to Clay. 'I'll run it back to Tallboys' Garage.'

Clay nodded his thanks to the Barchester officers and strolled calmly towards the Jaguar.

'Thank you, Sar'nt Booth,' he said, 'but I'll take care of this, if you don't mind.'

Booth's jaw dropped and the patrolmen grinned as Clay slipped into the driver's seat and let a hand fall on the gear lever. He adjusted his seat forward a little and reached for the ignition key.

'It may surprise you gentlemen to know', he said pleasantly, 'this is not the first time I've driven one of these.'

'Yes, well – take it easy, sir,' the Barchester driver cautioned. 'They go like a bat out of hell.'